MURRAY

PERRY'S NEST BOOK 4

KATHI S. BARTON

This is a work of fiction. Names, characters, places, and incidents are products of the author's imagination or are used fictitiously and are not to be construed as real. Any resemblance to actual events, locations, organizations, or persons, living or dead, is entirely coincidental.

World Castle Publishing, LLC
Pensacola, Florida

Copyright © 2023 Kathi S. Barton
Paperback ISBN: 9798891261204
eBook ISBN: 9798891261211
First Edition World Castle Publishing, LLC, December 8, 2023
http://www.worldcastlepublishing.com

Licensing Notes

Cover: Karen Fuller
Editor: Karen Fuller

Prologue

Murray didn't know what to think about the newly appointed town board members who were there as soon as he arrived at his parents' home. While they were standing around, talking to anyone who came by, and there were plenty of visitors at the home, he snuck his way into the large castle by pulling the shadows around him as he went to find his parents. He just happened to find his father first.

"Dad? What's with the news crews and police here? Has something happened?" Dad told him that it was a nightmare. "Dad, there are times when you think something is somewhat of a nightmare when it just takes a little adjustment here and there to fix. What's really going on?"

"The new board members, I'm sure you saw them, are saying they have decided to put a road through our land that will go right by the house with only mere inches to spare. And in that, they're going to have to tear down our home. I had no idea they were running a stupid road through — tell me, son, where would it go to or even, for that matter, come from? There is nothing beyond here but more of our land, and it just comes from the town that we mostly own as a starting point. They're not even going to — I'm not telling this well as I'm very upset. They only just sprung this on us this morning. And they're saying that the equipment will be here in the morning to tear it down. I've never — aren't they supposed to give notice of something like this? At least have a meeting with me? I'm in a fubble, son. A huge fubble."

"I'm not entirely sure what a fubble is, Dad, but let me see what is going on here." With the shadows drawn around him once again, Murray wandered around the yard and home to see what he could glean from other people's minds. Twice, he heard that someone thought that the mayor was going to be living in the castle once it was updated, and then he heard that once the road was started, it would finish up right at the castle gates and be used as a tourist attraction when the road funding would suddenly disappear. Since there was very little money for anything like a single parking space, much less a road, he believed that one more. His parents were being duped.

Murray only knew one person who could get to the bottom of things, and that was his good friend, Brad Kirk. The man was like a dog with a bone. Chewing on every inch of it until he got all the marrow or, in this case, information that he could out of it before he was ready to say that he had all there was to have. And he would have it, too. The man was a diligent investigator when someone asked for his help.

He'd been around for such a long time that Murray was surprised that he'd been buying up land not far from where his parents lived. Reaching out to him to see what he might be able to dig up, Kirk was just as happy to hear from him as he was contacting him.

"You're not going to believe this, but I read about this shit in this morning's paper. I even went back a few years looking online, and there isn't one mention of this road to nowhere going on. If what you're saying is, in fact, the truth of the matter, Hamish will need to be involved. Since he's king, no one can buy or sell land without giving

him first dibs on it. It's not his rule, but one that has been around for a long time. I mean, you can still inherit it from your father, but if you were wanting to sell, he gets to be the first to turn it down. I think it has something to do with the money owed to baby vamps that might turn up later to claim the land or something like that." Murray said that he remembered that law from a long time ago. *"I only just remembered it when I was looking into the land ownership. Also, neither the mayor nor the board members can simply buy up land that has been in a family for centuries by Eminent Domain by claiming that it's reasonably shown that the property is to be used for public purposes only. Also, they'd have to compensate them for all the land and the castle at fair market value. I don't think there is enough money in the entire town to show that they can do that, even with a loan from the state or country. I don't know how they'd be able to get someone to come in and value the land and the castle, but I would imagine that it would be in the hundreds of billions of dollars just for the castle and the lands around it. Doesn't that sucker sit on about fifty thousand acres?"*

He told him that his parents also owned more than half the land that the town was residing on, and they paid rent to his family to use the land for their government buildings as well as roads and homes.

"*The rents, which aren't extraordinarily high from the city for the rent they pay, has been behind for the last four or five years too.*" He thought of something. "*Could that be the reason this is going on? Do they want to get out of paying the rent they're being sued for? I know that the last time I was home, Dad had a law firm looking into just how to get the money from the cities.*"

"*I'll be there in a few days. Stall all you can. Call Hamish and let him know what is going on as well. He has the money and kingdom to toss around to get things going in the right direction.*" He told him about Cal and how he was now the king of all burin. "*Well, if that don't beat all. He should have been a long time ago if you were to ask me. All right, call him too. It might be funny to see a bunch of bears roaming around the land, scaring the shit out of people that have no right to anything that they're doing. This could be more fun than I thought it would be.*"

Murray made sure to call Cal first. He knew that if he were to call Hamish first, he'd never get off the phone with him. He'd want every detail about his family, including his brother and sister, and then he'd ask about his parents before he ever got to the point where he could tell him what was going on. Even then, he'd want details he wouldn't have until Brad got back to him. Cal was still laughing when he hung up with him, telling him that there was a fairly large burin right around there of about a thousand bears, and he'd have them roaming the property to keep it safe. Murray couldn't have asked for better news. Then he called Hamish.

After explaining to his wife as Hamish was taking care of some stupid shit—her words—with his new job, she'd help him out. She sounded like she was going to not just help him out but also she was going to have the best fun ever in helping him. Yes, Murray thought, he was going to enjoy this much better.

Thirty minutes after talking to Lander, he got a call from someone by the name of Rosie Thimble. She asked if she could speak to the man in charge; however, she asked if there was an FBI agent there, the highest ranking one. While he didn't know how to tell one from the other in the way of rank, he did find someone to help him with that.

He didn't walk away. It was his phone, after all. He could hear the woman's voice. She was screaming into the phone. The man listening on his end would say things like 'yes, sir' 'I'll get on that right now, sir' and other things that made him think that the woman on the other end had to be some ball buster to make a grown man sputter and spit like he was.

When the call ended, and the phone was handed back to him, the agent walked away. Murray was positive if the man had had a tail, it would have been right between his legs. Since Murray didn't know if she'd hung up or not, he said hello into his cell phone. She asked him who he was.

"Murray Phelps. This is my parent's home that is being invaded by the idiots." She agreed with him that they were all fucking idiots. "Can I ask you what your part in this is?"

"Yes. I'm FBI. And since about twenty minutes ago, I've been promoted to Agent in charge of this shit storm. Like, I don't have a million other things that I should be working on rather than a land dispute with some moron that thinks just because his brother-in-law has a job working at the White House—as a dishwasher, I might add, that he could help his family take over homes of people that have been around a hell of a lot longer than the fucking White House where he works has been. Fucking stupid people. I hate them all." He couldn't help it. He laughed. She wasn't just honest as hell, but she didn't pull any punches when talking to people, either. "You'd not think this was so funny if you were where I am right now, trying to get an autopsy done by exhuming a body only to find out that there is no fucking body, not even sandbags, to make the weight of the thing believable."

"Are you coming here to this shit storm?" She told him that she didn't have much else to do, so she had to go there and roll some heads. "I'd like to see that. I'm betting all my fortune that you're going to do a very good job of it. What is going to happen anyway?"

"If that dumb fuck I just talked to does what I told him, the mayor, his wife, two children as well as the secretary, her staff, as well as the police chief are going to be arrested. In addition to trying to accuse your father of being a vampire, which I do know that he is—defamation of character is a heavy fine when you're trying to take your family home because of racism." He asked her if her father was a vampire, then why would that be a reason to be called racist. "Sure, I don't care what your family is either, but the county seat can't write up a report about him being different, as in a vampire, in order to have him thrown off his land and his property—which they had no intentions of paying for, then that's against the law."

When she told him she had to go, he dejectedly hung up the phone. But he did mark her number in his caller ID with her name. In the event, he told himself that he had another question to ask her along the lines of asking her out to dinner or something.

The people that Rosie had mentioned had been arrested by the time he was in the yard again. Mom and Dad were sitting on the porch watching the events, too, when he sat down on the swing and joined them. A van pulled up about an hour later, and not only was it filled with more agents, but a woman dressed in jeans and a very skin-fitting blouse also got out too. The way she was talking, he just knew that this was the woman who had saved the day.

She didn't make her way up to the porch right away. Which he was fine with. Watching her ordering people around, once pulling out her gun and firing it into the ground, had him and his parents laughing. Apparently, the mayor thought of himself as well above a female FBI agent who carried a gun, and he was taken away in one of the city's new cruisers alone.

Hamish and his new mate also showed up. They didn't come up to the porch where they were before talking to two of the agents who had shown up with who he assumed was Rosie. She was pissed, every line of her beautiful body showed it, but once Hammy hugged her tightly in his arms, she seemed to calm down a bit. When she went back to the van, he thought for sure he was going to miss talking to her face-to-face when she reached in and pulled a large dog from the back.

The dog was hers. There was no doubt about it when he matched her step to step, never leaving her side without a lead on him. Joey, Murray heard her calling him, kept up with her, but never stopped looking around for whatever might hurt his mistress. Finally, she made her way to the house where he and his parents were.

Hamish introduced her as Cal's sister-in-law. Then he told her about his family's long history of being here in this spot. She was polite, very much so, but he could tell that she didn't like being held up when there was work to be done, but she tolerated it well. When he watched her turn her head when his father went to kiss her, he laughed again.

"You were the little shit on the phone." He said that was him. "You know, you could have told me that it's your family that I was helping. I could have had you or one of them taking care of the mayor. Did you know that he's been stashing cash on the upper floors of the library that his wife has been using for her office? They've been crooks for some time now."

"I don't live here with my parents any longer, so, no, I had no idea what was going on until I came here to visit my family." He put out his hand to touch her in the guise of a handshake. "My name is Murray Phelps. I have a lot of titles, too, but that should help me learn your name."

The moment that he touched his hand to hers, he felt a feeling roll over him akin to his skin being set on fire. Not only his skin but where her fingers were touching his. He could feel the iciness of her anger like it was his own. Closing his eyes to the onslaught of not only her anger but every memory that she'd ever had. He could only wonder what she was getting from him.

~*~

Cal had no idea what had happened to Rosie or Murray, but every time he looked at him, he would burst out laughing. Not only was he still unconscious, but his forehead was bleeding still, and he was sure that the old vampire had broken a couple of fingers trying to hold onto Rosie when she was blasted away, much like Warren told him that he had when meeting Lander for the first time. When Murray sat up in bed, yelling out Rosie's name, he laid him back on the bed and told him to calm down.

"Where is she? She's powerful." Cal said that he'd gotten that, too. "Where is she, Cal? I think she's my mate."

"According to her, and if I were you, I'd take this as gospel, she's not going to be anyone's plaything until she says so. Not to mention, being married or mated to a man that has no more sense than to get himself fixed up before being put to bed is going to expect her to baby and coddle him, and she'd rather stake you than to be around your whiney ass. What did you say to her when she helped you up off the floor?" He said he didn't remember that at all. "I'd start with that. It might, well, more than likely not go over better than you telling her you're her mate again. I think you've told her nearly a thousand times since the two of you were blasted apart."

Cal laughed again. "Now, what's so funny?" He laughed harder. "Tell me what you find so funny, or so help me. I'm going to kick your ass three weeks into next year."

"You. My god, Murray, how long has it been since we've been all together? Marshall isn't here yet, but he's on his way, and Hammy's grandda is having a grand time having all these beautiful women coming around all the time. He's just the same as he was all those years ago, too." Murray asked again where Rosie was. "She's working. I'll tell you now that she's a great nurse but a better doctor than I've ever met. Right now, she's working on something for the hospital that has needed attention for some time. She and her sister are also working at the Health Plex part-time until we can get it up and running better. It's doing well, but it needs some of the things that no one ever thinks about when they're putting together a place for people to get help. Understand?"

"Yes. Can I go and see her, or will that just be causing me more pain?" Cal told him he hadn't any idea as he tried very hard to stay on her good side. "Probably a smart move. The only times I've spoken to her, she seems to fly off the handle pretty easily."

"Usually, she doesn't. She's calm and cool. But when she's upset, there is no comparison to her anger. To say that she doesn't suffer fools easily is an understatement. When we hired a head of surgery for the clinic we're funding, he told her that she'd be better off being his secretary rather than an RN. He had no idea she was a better-qualified doctor than he was at being a man. I kid you not, Murray. She's got balls too. If I were her mate, I'd just step back and let her run the show. She's not much into cuddling, either. Just the opposite of Ruby, her sister. Though here lately, she's just as bad. I love them both."

Getting out of the bed for Murray seemed to be a lot more difficult than he thought it should have been for the man. Deciding to take him to the hospital to see Rosie seemed like a better idea, even if it was to have her pissed off. Whatever had zapped him when they touched seemed to have had no effect on Rosie at all but had seemingly all but drained Murray all the way to his toes.

On the way to the hospital, he pointed out some of the projects they were working on. The new grounds for the schoolyard were the best, he thought. While driving around, they came across his daughter with the babies, and he introduced Murray to them as well. By the time they were at the hospital, Murray was dozing off and on and didn't look all that well. Almost as soon as they entered the hospital, Murray asked for a wheelchair and for his mate. Reaching out to Rosie, she came to him quickly.

Taking him to her office, Cal stayed with the couple. He was worried. More worried than he had been about anything else in his life. Once he was wheeled into the office, the door was locked and the shades drawn. Hamish appeared in the office when Rosie simply stood in the middle of the room and shouted his name. One look at Murray, and he asked Rosie what she wanted to do.

"How the fuck am I to know what to do? You're in charge of shit. Fix him up so that he doesn't look like every horror picture show they've ever made about vampires. You're the ding dong in charge." Hamish glanced at him, then turned back to Rosie. Whatever she thought of, she wasn't the least bit happy about it. "Oh, you have got to be kidding me? He needs my blood? Mother fuck, I don't even want him, much less his munchers in my neck. That's what it is, isn't it? He's hungry, and I'm the only one who can feed him. Like I'm on the menu or some bull fucking shit as that."

"He's been hurt, or it might not be as — "

"I didn't hurt him, damn it. Whatever happened just happened. Why do I have to be the one that gets all eaten up because he wasn't smart enough to have a hardy meal before coming home to see his mom and dad?" Hamish said that if she didn't help him, he would die. "And if I say no, you're going to blame me for the rest of my life. Hell, even if you didn't, I would. All right, but no fucking around. I just want to feed him and send him on his way. I did point out to you earlier that I had a shit load of stuff to do today, and it's not going to be getting done while I'm hooked up to him like a shank of beef."

After explaining to her what needed to be done, she was no less pissed off about it. But she did make them promise not to leave them because she was afraid that he'd drain her dry. Which was a good argument. If he was this weak, then he was very hungry. With her being his mate and him nearly on death's doorstep, Murray might hurt Rosie without knowing it. Sitting on his lap facing him, Hamish opened a vein on her wrist for him to get a taste. Then, when he was ready to feed, he'd help her by opening the larger one in her throat. Yeah, Cal thought, this could be very dangerous for Rosie.

Once Murray took a few sips from Rosie's wrist, he took her throat. He had to keep reminding himself that in normal times, Murray wouldn't be this violent with his mate, but it took both him and Hamish to keep him from killing his mate. Once he had enough to heal himself, they asked Rosie to back away. They'd not realized how weak she was until she stumbled across the room and fell to the floor.

"We'll each give her a bit of our blood so that she'll be all right. He'll never forgive himself if he realizes what he's done to her." Cal said that he'd go first because of him not being a vampire and related to her. If that worked, Hamish wouldn't have to help Rosie out. Cal's blood was strong for being so old and King now, but she was still fading fast.

Hamish gave her a bit more than he thought he should have. But like Rosie had said, he would never forgive himself if he didn't help his friend's mate while she was down, especially after agreeing to help Murray.

It was several hours, and Hamish and himself giving both of them blood three more times. Whatever had happened, it wasn't anything either of them had encountered before. Murray woke up twice, asking for Rosie, and between him and Hamish, they got the big man close enough to Rosie so that they could touch. Rosie never woke up in all this time.

"What's happening?" Cal and Hamish told Lander what had happened and what they had done to save their lives. "Do you think that you'll change her too? Like you did me?"

"Honestly, I've never thought of that. I only

wanted her to get better." Hamish said he'd not be able to tell right away if she had, but he wasn't going to let it bother him if he did it. Or if she became a bear by all this. "No, I think you're right. She's going to live, right? I'll even take any abuse she wants to hand out to me if she's around to do it."

The three of them watched over the couple for the next several days. They were able to take them to Hamish's home and put them in a room where the sunlight wouldn't bother them. They did find out that Rosie was now a vampire quite by accident because her skin burned badly when they were thinking of what room to put her in. In addition, they were able to get more help watching over them. Grandda didn't have any idea what had happened either, but whatever it was, they were getting better daily.

Ten days after they were blasted, it was Rosie who woke up first. She didn't seem to be terribly upset with finding herself in the big bed with Murray but did get up and go back to her house for a shower and a change of clothing or two. She also brought some toys for Joey to play with.

He'd never left her side while they were all watching over them but to go out and come back in after a bathroom break. Cal was worried about him because he wouldn't eat much but hoped that since he was in such good shape, it wouldn't harm him too much. He knew just how much the dog meant to Rosie, and she'd be terribly upset if anything were to ever happen to the guy.

After she returned with fresh clothing and her hair still damp, she asked what had happened. Cal knew better than to give her half-truths, so he told her straight up what had happened and what they knew. She took being a vampire all right, he thought, but she was concerned with Murray.

"Will he be all right?" Cal told her that he seemed to be getting stronger every hour since she woke up. "Is that a big deal? I mean, I know that I have some magic in me, thanks to you, but will it give him the willies when he finds out that I'm like him? A vampire?"

"I don't think he'll care overly much just knowing that you're alive. But it's been a very long time since I've seen Murray, so he might not be the same guy he was when we parted ways all those years ago. But I know if anyone can handle him, it would be you." She thanked him. "What else can I tell you? You've got some of my blood, too. And as you knew, before this all started, I was bruin King, so I haven't any idea what my stronger blood would have done to you. Oh, your sister will be over later with the babies and Missy. She took them to get some dinner out because they were so worried about you. So had Joey."

Like he knew they were talking about him, the dog picked up his pink pig and held it in his mouth while looking at them both. When Rosie scratched him on the head, they both let go of a huge sigh of relief. It was normal to be petted again after so long, he supposed, but these two were so good together.

"I don't know what I'm supposed to do now." Cal told her that he wasn't sure what she meant. "I don't know, jackass. Do I have to be here with him all the time? Will he want another feast when he wakes up? I don't fucking know."

"You could ask me." They both turned to look at Murray when he spoke. "I don't think I've been up and around for a bit. Right now, I'm feeling like I've been run over. What the hell is going on?"

"You've been resting." Cal stood up before laughing. "I'll leave you with your mate. Oh, by the way, she's been changed into a vampire. Maybe even a little bit of bear. So tread carefully. I don't think she's fully aware of what went on with her body either."

Cal left them there after that. He was still laughing when he got home, where his own family was hanging out. After being given a fashion show with the things that were purchased, he went to the sublevels to take a long, much-needed nap. It had been just too hard on him the last couple of weeks.

Chapter 1

Rosie wasn't sure how she felt about her new life. *New* was an understatement of how she was feeling and doing now. Not only had she been turned into a vampire, but she had a lot of the characteristics of a bear shifter, too. Reaching down to pet Joey when he whined a little, assuring him that she was fine, she leaned back on her chair and stared blindly at the computer some more.

Her sister Ruby was certainly happy. And she deserved it more than most, Rosie thought. She had three children, one almost fifteen and two four months old. And a baby on the way. Rosie would have been tearing her hair out, but Ruby, as usual, was taking it well and making it work for her. Smiling when she thought of Missy, her oldest, she couldn't help but be a bit jealous of that one. Missy, like the infants, had been adopted by her sister and brother-in-law Cal this winter, and she was keeping them all on their toes as much as the babies.

Frowning, she thought of her own mate, Murray. He'd nearly died when he first met her. Since neither of them had ever expected to find their other halves—actually, she'd had no desire to find hers—Murray hadn't fed his beast, the vampire, before helping his parents out with a problem, and he couldn't feed from anyone else after meeting her.

Then, when she agreed to allow him to munch at her neck, something that still made her shiver to this day, he'd nearly killed her by taking too much. If not for Cal, a bear shifter, and Hamish, the king of vampires, giving her some of their rich blood, she might well have died too. As it was, she and Murray had been laid up resting for almost two weeks before they'd been able to get up and around. Now that they were both healthy, they'd been avoiding each other since.

They did live in the same house together. It was a big fucker that she loved, and because of that, they'd been able to skirt around being a 'couple' since they'd moved in together. She had her life, and he had his. So far, she thought it was working out well for the two of them. Also, her busy schedule was keeping her away from home for almost sixteen hours every day. Rosie had no idea what Murray did for a living or, for that matter, what he did while she was at work. Her cell phone ringing had her reaching for it, barely holding onto her temper when she did.

"Are you going to bite my head off or listen to what I have to tell you?" Ruby. Their conversation from yesterday still a painful place in her heart. She told her that she'd listen. "Good. Murray is at his parents' home, trying his best to get through some of the things that you should be helping him with. Also, they're speaking to an attorney about the things that came up when the mayor of their town decided that he wanted to live in the castle."

"What would I do to help him? It's his family." Ruby pointed out that they were hers now, too. "I don't think they like me overly much. I'm not saying that because I don't want to go, but his mom is sort of snarky to me all the time, and I've been good at keeping my mouth shut. You know how hard that is for me. But I only showed up there yesterday, and she got pissy about what I was wearing. What was wrong with my jeans and T-shirt. Nothing, that's what."

"Was it clean?" She asked her what she meant. "I know for a fact that you've been doing autopsies for the state a lot, something about backlogs. So, was the shirt clean and free of blood? And maybe other parts of the bodies you're working on? You do remember that they're vampires, don't you? I mean, you might stink of old blood."

"I didn't think of that." She felt her temper rise a little. "Then why the hell didn't she just say, you stink? Wouldn't that have been the polite thing to do? Instead of asking me what I'm wearing? Christ, I hate when people don't just say what they're thinking."

"I'd be afraid to be honest with you about your smell, too, when you're snapping and biting at people all the time. Didn't we just talk about this yesterday? How, even now, Missy doesn't want to be around you?" That hurt Rosie more than her sister being mad at her. "You're going to have to make it up to her, or you're going to be missing a good niece and friend."

"I will. I promise. I didn't know anything about the school she wanted me to look at with her, and I was busy. Can't I be in a bad mood when I'm at work, and she comes there for advice?" Before she would let her sister answer, Rosie answered herself. "No, I can't. I have been letting my stress get the — what the fuck am I supposed to do with a mate, I ask you?"

Ruby didn't say anything. Rosie had asked this same question daily, if not hourly, of Ruby since she'd found herself mated to him. When the tears started to fall again, Joey, her wonderful companion and dog, laid his head on her leg and whimpered again. Petting him made her feel marginally better but not enough to get on with her day.

"I've been sitting here since seven-thirty this morning just staring at my computer. I've gotten nothing done. No reports filed. There are a stack of files here that I need to get loaded into the computer that won't take me long, but I just keep not doing it. I'm second-guessing myself at every turn. Not about work but just life. Ruby, it took me thirty minutes standing in the grocery to figure out that I didn't fucking want a salad for dinner but a steak and trimmings. But you know what I did? I bought six of those bagged-up salads so that I could eat that instead. Why, I ask you? Why did I do that? They're going to be rotten by the time I get around to them. What—"

"Hush." She snapped her mouth closed so quickly that it hurt her teeth a little. "I'm talking to

Murray about something."

She wanted to ask her if it was about herself but didn't. Ruby wanted to know, and she didn't. So, waiting on her sister, she opened the first file and started working on it on the computer. Being behind was something that she hated, and worse, when she was the reason that she was behind and not because of someone else's crappy work ethic. Rosie was done with the first file and working on the second when her sister came back on the line.

"This is stupid, you know that, don't you? He wants to know if you'll come to his parent's home so that they can have a nice visit with the two of you. Why am I the go-between? You should be with him, Rosie. Not hanging out at the hospital...what are you doing at the hospital anyway?" She told her. "Oh. Well, since you've not given him any idea what you're doing, he hasn't any idea that you're doing autopsies out of the ass and writing up findings about them. Didn't Launder say that she'd help with that?"

"She did help me. That's why I'm able to write up the reports that go with each body. But what you don't realize is that I have to go over all of our notes like I've started fresh on the bodies. It's draining to me." She let the tears fall, knowing that her sister would pounce on her if she were to know about them. "I'm exhausted all the time, and I'm working to make sure that crimes are being taken care of. You know, he could have asked me what my plans are instead of asking you to be the go-between."

Ready to close up her computer and go home and hide again, she screamed when Murray suddenly appeared in the room. Simply hanging up the call with her sister, Rosie stood up, going around her desk. The slap to Murray, even though she did it, was as much a shock to her as it looked as if it had been to him.

"Why are you involving my sister in us? Not that there is an us as far as I can see, but I don't have time for you whining to her about me. You have something to say to me, then say it, damn it. I'm fucking out of my league here trying to be someone that I've never been before." He asked her what that was. "I fucking don't know. A vampire? A mate to one? Did you know that yesterday I was taking a walk to work, and I was suddenly this fucking bear. It took me over an hour to figure out how to get home again to go back to being human. No one told me how I'm supposed to feel after being a vampire that I never counted on. Also, I was terrified that I was going to drink blood from one of the bodies that I was working on because I'm a fucking vamp—"

When he jerked her body to his, pulling her body flush with his much more muscled one, she held onto his shoulders as he studied her face. When he started to lower his head to her mouth, at least that's what she thought he was doing, all of her body seemed to wake up. Her mouth became different, and she felt the fangs that she'd never seen before moving. Murray touched his lips to hers but didn't deepen the kiss as she had hoped. He just stared at her, looking into her eyes like he was looking for a flaw.

~*~

Murray thought that she was pure perfection. The more he looked at her, into her somewhat, the more he could see why he loved her so very much. Dipping his head to hers again, taking just a little more of her, she nipped at his lower lip and brought his blood to her mouth. He moaned as he brought her head to his neck and held her there.

"I've been avoiding you because I want you so desperately. I'm terrified of harming you again." She said that he'd not harmed her before. "But I did. I nearly killed you when I'd gotten ill. I should have...I don't know what I might have done differently. I'd not fed. My parents had called me while I was out and about. They were...Dad is usually one to overreact about things, but once I got to him, it was actually worse than even he thought. The town was going to take our ancestral home and all of our land."

Rosie pulled away, but not to the point where he couldn't touch her. She watched his face as he explained that the mayor had wanted to take the home to bring in more revenue for the town. Mostly his own pockets. The entire time that he explained to her why he'd not fed before meeting her, she stared up at him. Finally, he ended it by telling her that he was afraid of nearly draining her again. That he'd not meant to do it at all the first time but he had been out of his head with hunger.

"You could have told me. They could have told me that, too." He nodded, saying that Hammy and Cal hadn't realized just how long it had been. "If you're going to tell me that you were starving yourself for a totally mental reason, I'm going to fucking murder you where you stand." Murray laughed. He just couldn't help it.

"No. I promise you. It was simply because I

hadn't thought about it. Or when I did, something else came up. I'm sure with your work ethic, you've done the same thing. Gotten to the point where you needed to take a power nap to go on with a job." She told him that she had, but she'd not drained anyone because of it. "No. I would imagine you'd not. But I am sorry that I hurt you. I didn't know what I was doing when I did it."

"Thank you for that. Not that I was all that concerned about it. We're both fine and filled up. You are filled up, aren't you?" He said that he wasn't hungry but never fulfilled of her. "I'm assuming that's you being romantic. I'm not much of a romancer. I like things to be straight up, and…are you going to kiss me? I haven't any idea why, but the thought of you kissing me is making me wet with need."

"Christ, woman." Standing now, Murray looked down at her and smiled. He could feel his fangs lengthen with need, his eyes darkening with it. Licking her lips, she looked up at him and ran her finger down his chest to his erection before she looked back up at his eyes.

"Take off your pants for me, Murray. I want to see your cock before you bury it in me." He groaned and started to unbuckle his belt. His movements were slow and deliberate. He was teasing her, and she was too needy to appreciate it, he thought.

Sitting up, she moved his hands out of her way and began working the buttons on his jeans open and kissed each inch of his skin as she exposed him as she lowered in front of him. His hard cock lay to the side, and working her finger over the rigid shaft, she moved it to the opening of his pants. Murray felt his eyes rolling to the back of his head. When it was where she had wanted it, she pulled his briefs down and licked the purple head as she continued to open the last button.

"Christ, woman. Your mouth needs to take me, now."

Moving the pants down over his ass and just below his balls, she cupped him from the rear and opened her mouth wide over him, taking him into her heat.

He knew that he was wide, she could barely hold him all, and the crown was so thick that it took her two tries to fit him into her mouth. Pulling back, he growled. Murray watched her taste all of him and licked her way down his vein to the dark nest of curls. She had shown him this in her projected images to him and did not realize how well she had imagined him until then.

His fingers laced in her hair, and he guided her back to the head. The stream of pre cum nearly had him come with anticipation, and she lapped it into her mouth with a hungry suckle. He tasted his blood, hot and spicy, as he bit down on his own lips, trying very hard not to hurry her nor make her stop.

Wrapping her hand around him, she began to pump him hard as she took him into her mouth again. Over and over, she swirled her tongue over him, teasing the tiny eye with the tip of her tongue, moaning when she felt more of him spill into her hot mouth.

"I want to come now, come down your throat, but I want to feel your body come all over my cock too. Stop now, baby, before I spill my seed this way again."

Reluctantly she took her mouth off his cock and lapped once more at the head for another taste. Rosie sat on the edge of her desk, careful of the paperwork and computer there. When he reached down and took off her jeans, it was all he could do to hold back long enough to look at her. She was soaking wet with need, and he could smell her perfumed want surrounding them both. When she was naked, he stood over her and looked at every inch of her.

"You're beautiful. I don't know if I can be gentle this time. My need to be in you is overwhelming. I want to fuck you until you scream, till we both scream."

"Do it. Fuck me hard, Murray. Please?" She opened her legs wide and let him see how badly she wanted him; her pussy was drenched and needy. Reaching down, she opened her nether lips wider and began to play with her clit while he watched. Murray knew she was only making him harder, but Christ, he thought, her body needed to come when he did.

Murray felt her move her hands, and before she could sit up to see what he was doing, his tongue pushed inside of her. Suckling him for those precious few moments and then playing with herself had made him too close, and her tongue threw him into a tailspin and out of control.

"Murray, please. Now, please." She screamed as she came, her hips bucked, nearly knocking him off her. Panting hard and wanting more, he grabbed a handful of her hair and pulled her up to his mouth. Even as he settled his cock at her entrance, she wrapped her legs around his hips and surged up, hard and fast, taking him deep inside of her.

He slammed into her as she rocked up again, not holding back at all but taking all that she'd give him. Rosie came again, her body tightening around his thickness; the pain/pleasure of him being so long and wide was amazing to them both.

Rocking into her again, he felt her still for a moment, then rock again, harder this time as he came inside of her. Over and over, he pulsed his hot cum into her. Over and over, he cried out her name as he did.

Finally, he collapsed on top of her. And just when he thought he was getting too heavy, he rolled to the floor somewhat clumsy, taking her with him.

Murray sat up slightly, almost too tired to move, and looked at her. Her small fangs biting into her lower lip were sexy for him. They were small, as he'd noticed, but they were sharp, too, like small daggers. And for as much as he wanted her to bite him, to feed from him, Murray knew that the two of them needed to talk. To get themselves in a better position of being mates than they had so far. He saw candy wrappers on her desk from his angle on the floor. Looking at her, he asked her if she was doing all right. If she needed anything from him. Shaking her head, she got up off his lap and pulled her pants back on.

"No. I mean, I can eat if I want. I've discovered that. The sun does bother me, but so long as I stay out of it during the hottest part of the day, I'm all right in dealing with a little red skin." She sat back down at the computer when she was dressed. "I don't know what to do."

Lying back on the carpet, he pulled his own pants up. Not bothering with zipping nor snapping them closed, he pulled the chair that had been knocked over by them upright and sat across from her. He asked her what she meant by not knowing what to do.

"Your parents don't like me. That's all on me. Ruby pointed out that I stink of old blood." He didn't say anything. "So they don't like me. Is that what you're telling me?"

"No. I thought you were just venting. And yes, you do smell like old blood, but that's because of me, not what you're wearing. I don't think so, anyway. You smell that way because you're mated to a very old vampire. As for not liking you? That's not true either. You've not allowed them to get to know you, so that's why they're standoffish with you." She nodded and lowered her head, telling him that she was sorry. "Don't be sorry, Rosie. Do something about it. They're good people. My dad is a little absent-minded, but he is excited to get to know you. Mom, well, she told me that she's never been around a daughter-in-law, but she'd heard stories about how they never get along, and she's afraid that you will just not like her because of that. Will you come to have dinner with me tonight with them? We can all eat, but it's not as fulfilling as it would be for a human. It would be nice to just sit around and get to know one another too."

"Why did you ask Ruby to ask me?" He told her. "Oh. I guess that is a good reason. I do tend to get buried in my work and get snappish when I'm too busy to ask…actually, Murray, I think that I'm snappish all the time lately. It's like I have something to prove or something like that. Is it because of work? I don't know. I'm just not used to being this pissed off all the time. It hurts my head when I'm like that all the time."

"It's more than likely because we're apart." She looked at him, pissed. "If I held your hand right now, how do you think that would make you feel? Better? Worse? How?"

He put out his hand and let her take it. When she curled her fingers over his, he felt not just his beast calming, but his body seemed to have calmed a great deal as well. She looked about as confused as he'd ever seen a woman.

"I feel like I'm settled. Like I've been balanced out. Like I have someone I can depend on right this moment." Rosie looked at him. "I don't feel pissed off anymore either. Like you've taken some of the burden from me from whatever I was feeling. Are you fucking kidding me? This is all I needed all along? Christ, it makes me sound like I'm some sort of pussy, don't you think?"

"I think it sounds wonderful. Like a bride of a vampire and all mine." He kissed the back of her hand before she got pissy with him again. "All right. You didn't answer my question. Would you like to go have dinner with my parents tonight? Also, after that, we can work with some of the magic that you got by bonding with me. Not to mention whatever you have from Cal. Since you've figured out that you can become a bear, we'll set that aside for now."

"Would it be all right if we sort of table a lot of things for now?" Murray asked her what she meant by that. "Well, I'm in over my head with a lot of things right now. I know that I can do what I need to do with magic, but I'm terrified of trying. I'm so used to being only able to depend on myself for things I don't know what to do about asking for help. If you could show me a few things about this overwhelming magic that I seem to have, I'd feel a good deal better and might be able to use it to get this work done."

"You mean computer work." She nodded. "Call Robin to help you. Or I can if you don't have a connection yet. She figured out easily that she could simply tell a computer what she wanted it to do, and that worked for her. I think that if you were to get her to tell you or even see if you can do it yourself, it might help me out, too. I have a lot of shit that I need to computerize that my parents have. Like records that date back centuries before I was born."

After talking to Robin for a few minutes, he saw that Rosie was able to do what she'd done and simply tell the computer what she wanted done. It was easy for her to get the stuff input on the computer. As he watched her make a spreadsheet, something that the FBI wanted from her, he realized that he could use the same spreadsheet for the things that his parents had. Mostly, it was lineage, but it would work for just about any input that he could think of.

After leaving the office, they ended up in the parking lot of the hospital. He hadn't arrived by car, but it was a big enough open space that they could bounce, what Rosie called it, from place to place. It was another bit of magic that he was able to help her with, and she made him feel like a hero when she hugged and kissed him for his advice.

The first thing that Rosie did when she was in the presence of his parents was to tell them how very sorry she was. Mom didn't know what to do when Rosie also admitted that she'd been pushing him away because she was terrified of making a mistake. The mistake being that she'd fuck up so badly that they'd stake her in the middle of the night.

"We'd never...oh my goodness, child, we'd never do that. I don't even think that we can because of you being a relative now." Dad laughed after telling Mom that wasn't a good thing to say. "No, I guess it's not. But no, I'd never...I hope that I'd be a better mother-in-law than that. Goodness."

They settled in the living room with Joey there, too, and talked about all sorts of things having to do with the two of them. Mom pulled out an old tome, giving it to Rosie so that she could read it over. It was about his family line, the only book that they had that also mentioned magic that the family had, too.

"We're a pure line of vampires." Rosie asked his dad if he was disappointed that she wasn't a born vampire. "Oh no. Not at all, dear. I don't mean this to sound terrible but having a pure line means a lot of relatives, some too close being married to each other. We've not had a lot of that through the years, but only because we've been careful. However, it does happen. You understand. Fresh blood and all." Dad looked at him and then shook his head. "I sometimes don't allow my head to think before my mouth opens."

"I do that all the time. I find that if I have to think too much about what I want to say, then I'm in the wrong group of people. My sister is forever making me watch my mouth around the kids. I can do it, but I get too frustrated about talking and just shut up. I'm reasonably sure that Missy, the oldest of her kids, has heard way worse." Dad and Mom had both heard about Missy and her sister. "Missy has finally come to terms with her sister's death. Beth committed suicide because she'd been treated so terribly from birth until she died. Both girls had been."

"Yes, we heard about those poor little things. I'm so glad that Cal and your sister are raising them. They'll be all right with such a loving family holding onto them." Mom looked at him and smiled. "Your dad and I have been thinking that we'd like to move into a house and leave the castle to you and Rosie. With the magic that the house has, it would be wonderful for the two of you to live here and raise a family, if that's in the future."

"We'd need to talk about it." Murray felt Rosie squeeze his hand and thought that they'd be moving in. "Mom, you'd not be moving far away, would you? I mean, I don't know that I'd be too happy with that."

"Me either, to be honest. If we do decide to have children, and we've not talked about that either, I haven't a clue how to raise a child, much less a vampire." Rosie looked at his dad then. "Mr. Phelps, what is your opinion of living close to the two of us?"

"Please call me Hamilton. And this lovely creature is my wife, Lilith. But I'd be thrilled to live close enough that we could see you two daily. Not all day, mind you, but just to be able to know that the two of you are around would make me feel so much better. When this thing with the castle started up, I was afraid that Murray wasn't going to be able to come to us. It scared me to no end to think that everything that we've worked for—and it is a considerable amount—that the city nearby would simply be able to take it from us. I'm so glad that I called, you know, but I was afraid."

"I would be as well if someone were to try and take my wealth from me. Even my family. That would include my dog. Joey and I have been through a great deal together, along with my sister Ruby. Just the thought of losing a way to take care of them makes me nervous, too." Dad asked if he could pet Joey. "Of course you can. He can be a lot at times, especially when he's playing outside, but he's been so calm lately."

Dad enjoyed playing with the dog so much that he asked to take him to the yard. When he left them, with several of the toys that Rosie had on her all the time, Mom looked at the two of them and told them that they'd made his day.

"That's all he talked about was your puppy. We've never tried to have a pet when we were younger, but seeing how that pup of yours dotes on you, well, it made him sort of jealous." Murray asked

Mom if Dad wanted a dog now. "I'm not sure. One minute, he says he does, and the next, he's afraid that he'd not do it right or something. You talk to him, Rosie. See what you can get out of him for a puppy. I think we'd both love having one around to take walks with."

Murray was going to see about getting his parents a dog. Joey had made such an impression on Hammy that he'd gotten one, too. Even though he'd said that he wouldn't, it would die before he did, he decided that having one for the kids would be special to them. It would be good for his parents because, just as his mom had said, to take walks with. That would be something that he could work with, too, making it so that older vampires — or hell, any creature — could enjoy a pet too.

Chapter 2

Rosie decided that she was going to talk to Missy. The little girl had gone through a great deal, but she was smart and had a great head on her shoulders. Going to her room, she opened the door and found her sitting on the floor crying. Rosie didn't ask her what was going on but sat on the floor across from her and stared at her. The look she got had her nearly laughing, but she decided that she'd more than likely get a bloodied lip, so she just smiled at her niece.

"You should knock when you enter someone else's room, you know. It's the polite thing to do." Rosie told her that it wasn't in her to be polite. "Yeah, I got that too. You're mean to me a lot and I don't like that either. Tell me whatever it is that you came here for, and then go away. I'm not in any kind of mood to put up with you today, Aunt Rosie."

"Yeah, I got that figured out. Sort of, anyway. I needed to be near Murray. That's what was pissing me off all the time. I'm getting this vampire shit figured out, but some of it is just stupid. Go figure. Anyway, what the fuck is wrong with you? Are you having a shitty day or something? So am I if you want the truth. I came to you for advice." She told her to go away. "You know that's not going to happen. What's wrong with you?"

"Today, Bethy would have been sixteen. She would have been able to get her driver's license and taken her children on rides. But she's dead." Rosie snorted, and Missy looked at her, pissed off more than she did before. "You know, you can be nice to me once in a while. I'm hurting right now."

"I am being nice. I didn't knock you around for saying something so stupid, did I? Bethy wouldn't have been able to get her license because she wasn't going to be able to get her parents to sign for her to. Not to mention, that would have been how they would have found you both. I don't know why, but I just have a feeling that she wouldn't have wanted to get her license anyway. She seemed, I don't know, Missy, too above wanting to learn to drive. What's really bothering you? You know as well as I do that you're not upset because she didn't get to drive. Tell me so that I can get on with my questions for you."

"I keep thinking about how she killed herself. The pain that she must have been in taking her fork and stabbing her wrists until they were beyond fixing. Stabbing it into her babies and nearly killing them so that they'd die as well. What sort of sick mind does that to innocent children?" Rosie could tell that wasn't the question that Missy wanted to ask her, but she was pissed off, and it sort of spilled out. "Then there is the fact that she had planned it all along. Even including me in her plans of people dying. Why? What did I do to her that she thought my being dead was the only way to go? Long enough for her to have written out what she wanted done and stuff." Rosie asked her what she thought was wrong with her sister. "Honestly? I don't have any idea what would have made her think and do those things? From being treated the way that she had been. I was being raped and hurt, too, but I didn't want to die. She was sick in the head. Right?"

"Absolutely." She could see that she'd shocked her niece. Which she was glad for. This was a serious conversation. "But then, having had been raped her entire life, and I'm talking more than likely from infancy, made her not be able to think of herself as anything but a damaged person. Someone said that to her, and it stuck in her head. And she was. However, she didn't talk about it. Not with you, not with anyone either when she arrived here. If not for you speaking up, we might not have known anything about her. Because there were people here that she could talk to about it. Only you spoke, and you were just as damaged as she was. However, and you have to remember this when you think of how sick she was, you were lucky enough not to have been having a child or children so young."

"You're saying that I was lucky?" Rosie told her that she was and still was. "How do you figure that?"

"Don't make me have to smack you around, Missy. What do you think you'd be doing right now if Cal and my sister hadn't taken you in? Where would you be?" Missy said she'd be living on the streets. "No. You'd be dead."

Missy started crying, saying that she sometimes wished that she was dead. That she didn't feel like she had anything or anyone to live for. Rosie pulled her to her and into her lap, holding onto her while she told her that she wakes up in the middle of the night sometimes thinking that very thing. Rosie asked her what she did when she was having those feelings. How she coped with it.

"I go see the kids. Sometimes, if they're waking up, I pick them up and hold them tightly. I don't tell them about their mom. I'm ashamed for them to—I know they can't understand me, but I don't want to ruin their childhood by telling them about what she'd done to them." Rosie didn't say anything but let her talk. However, she was thinking that this kid needed help. "The doctor that I'm seeing told me that I'm focusing too much on my life and should be thinking of the people around me and what they'd think if I followed through on it. To be honest with you, Aunt Rosie, I don't give two fucks what everyone thinks. I just can't stand to be alive anymore. No one is going to love me like Dad does Mom. Like Murray does you. I'm terrified of men. I'm going to be alone for the rest of my long and miserable life. And it's not fair."

Missy sobbed while Rosie cried with her. It *was* unfair, and she was also thinking that the doctor she was seeing wasn't doing her a bit of good. Not that she knew a great deal about head doctors, but this bitch sounded like she wasn't listening to her niece.

When Missy calmed down, she looked up at her. Rosie could tell that she was hurting, but she knew very little about how to make her feel better. So, she did what she thought was right for the little girl.

"I know you have an idea what I did in the service. So I'm going to skip over the part where I have to explain how I got to be on the front line of a very terrible situation on a daily basis." Rosie said she did know. "Good. Keep that in mind when you think you can get around me in something. Anyway. There was this serviceman named Hardin. Last name. I never knew first names. That's important. We were being bombarded with fire while I was trying to stitch this guy up that had gotten his ass shot up. He thought that he was above being killed because he was an American soldier. Idiot. Hardin was assisting me. Really all he was doing was annoying the fuck out of me by bitching about how he wasn't supposed to be here. He was making sure that I was safe while operating. Some of the team, mostly nurses and guys pushing gurneys, were going up closer to the line, and I was behind for the stragglers. This idiot said that he'd had a life before being put on this team that was forever being shot at. He kept complaining about how his girl back home didn't care for him being so far away either. I found out later that he was there as a last-minute replacement for me. They should have done a better job of having someone stay with me than this fool. If you would have asked me, I think he was off his noodle too far to be in the service at all, much less with a weapon. While I was finishing up on the guy that I was stitching up, Hardin started in on me again. I told him to shut the fuck up. He was giving me a fucking headache. Then he got pissy and told me that I was a fucking cunt. That I shouldn't have been there because I was a woman, and I should have been home taking care of babies and shit. Before I could stomp his ass because that's what he needed, he pulled out his service weapon and shot the man I had just saved in the fucking head. Just like that. Then he pointed the gun at me. I did the same with my weapon."

"My goodness. I would have pooped my pants." She said that she nearly had but didn't show him that. "Go on. I'm sure that there is a good ending to this."

"There isn't. There rarely is a good ending when there are guns involved. He shot me. Not in the head but in the chest. Twice. I had been able to get off a shot, too, and hit him in the heart. As he was falling back, dead, that's when he shot me the second time." Rosie thought of how the man had been able to get off a second shot because of his finger clenching up around the trigger. "When his shit in his tent was cleaned out to be sent back to his parents, they found a note. It was about how he'd been the one who had shot the man I was working on. That he'd wanted to be sent home and was hoping that would work. He also talked about how he'd been having sex with the same serviceman and was afraid that he was going to tell on him and that it would get back to his parents. They'd hate him, as they'd already spent a great deal of money on making him not *gay*. He also mentioned how I wasn't even nice enough to learn his first name, and that made him feel less of a man, too."

Neither of them said anything, but Rosie was thinking about the young man who had nearly killed her. And how long it had taken her to get well enough to be sent home for some rest. Upon getting home, neither her doctor nor her sister had figured out that she'd been nearly dead not two weeks before. Rosie had never told that story to anyone before, not even the head doc that she'd been assigned to talk to. Some things were just better unsaid, Rosie thought.

"He was damaged, too." Rosie told her that he was. "Do you suppose if he'd gotten the right help, he would have been all right? That if he'd been able to talk to someone, better than the woman that I am talking to, that he would have been able to cope with life?"

"I don't know the answer to that, Missy. To be honest with you, there was help he could have gotten while in the service. But he didn't ask for it." She nodded and kept her head on her chest as she held her. "Do you think that the woman that you're talking to, honestly now, do you think that she's helping you?"

"No. Not nearly as much as you just have. You just told me that there are other people out there who are worse off than I am. And that if I don't get up off my ass and get help, I'm going to be shooting people in the head, then myself when I've emptied the gun." She looked up at her. "Right?" Rosie laughed.

"If you tell my sister that's how I helped you, she's not going to allow me to ever talk to you again, but I guess that's what I was doing." Hugging the child, Missy moved away from her but still close enough that she could hold her hand. "I'm not saying that there are always people out there that have it worse than you did. Christ, honey, I don't know that I'd want to meet the person who had a more fucked up life than you and Beth did. However, you're going to hopefully come out on top of this where Beth didn't because you know how to ask for help. And have someone that you can talk to about it. Not that bitch that you're seeing right now but someone else. What's her name anyway?"

"I'm not going to tell you that. You'd hunt her down and...you know what, I don't want to even think about what you'd do or say to her. I'll get someone else to help me. And I will." Rosie told her that when she had those thoughts again for her to call her, and she'd talk to her. "No. I mean, I might call you, but you'd not talk. You'd knock me around a little, and while that would help, Mom would be pissed at you."

"She more than likely would." The two of them sat there before she remembered why she'd come to find the girl. "I need your help. I'm supposed to make my office more user-friendly. You might ask yourself why I'd want anyone in my office, and you'd be right on that. I don't. But I might need to bring in someone from the outside and give them information. The biggie was conducting an interview or something.

Right now, I don't even have a desk. I mean, I do have one, but it's only a long table with a laptop on it. I have one of those balls that you're supposed to sit on that is going to make you feel better about exercising or some shit. It's annoying to have to keep my balance on it all the time, but I suppose that's the point. Right? Anyway, I need some stuff on the wall, a desk, and some other shit. They suggested that I have my awards and diplomas on the walls with some serene pictures. I don't even know what would be considered serene. Can you help me? I'll pay for everything and for you helping me. But I don't even know where to start with this shit."

"They mean like pictures of your family or pictures of vacation spots that you would have gone on. Have you ever taken a vacation?" She told her about her camper. "We'll do that this summer, right? You and me? I think that would be a blast."

"Sure. We'll go to the ocean. You ever been there?" Missy said she'd not been anywhere. "Then we'll make it happen. But in the meantime, can you help me with my office?"

"I'd love that." After asking Ruby if she could help her with finding a desk that would work, she suggested that they start with the storage barn that

Hammy had. They were still digging around in the place when Murray joined them.

~*~

Murray had to laugh every time he thought of Missy's face when her aunt put her hand on the desk that they'd found, and it disappeared. It was in her office, the three of them discovered later, but it was as if the kid had never seen magic before. But they were able to get Rosie's office outfitted with every piece of furniture that she needed in very little time and effort. Rosie asked what Missy needed to do now.

"If I take you to the office supply store, are we going to get arrested for stealing? I mean, it is a good possibility that if you make things disappear, we'll end up in jail." Rosie, good-natured about it, told her that they'd just have to wait and see. "I've been in jail before. It's not a place that I'd like to end up that my parents have to come and get me from."

"Yeah, I've been there too. You're right. It's not a good place to hang out. But I'll keep my hands to myself." They were all in such a good mood that he found himself laughing more than he had in a long time. "All right. And this picture thing. You said you can make that work, too? I can't wait to see some of the pictures you showed me blown up."

The idea was for some of the pictures of the kids to be put in Rosie's office so that she'd have them close. The store they were going to could not just blow them up for Rosie but put them into frames, too. As soon as Rosie showed Missy her nameplate that the FBI had made up for her to put in her new office, it was a free-for-all for you young girl putting things in their cart that matched the beauty of the placard.

The pictures were beautiful. The place had this thing where they could mount the pictures on glass and be hung on the wall. There were a few pictures of the kids, even Missy, but also of the ones that he took on their way here from Florida. He learned about the vacation that the three of them were going to take — he'd been invited at the last minute and was happy that he'd been included. But once they were finishing up in the office, he had to admit that it looked a good deal better than he'd thought it would when it took them all four trips to get all the items in the room.

"I love this. I mean, it's really foo-foo and all, but I love it. It looks like someone else's office." Missy was about to bust a button. She was so proud of being complimented by her aunt. He even told her how much he liked it and might have to do his at the clinic. "You really should do this, kid. It looks like I could have someone in here, and they'd not think that I was some kind of slob."

The three of them ended up having dinner together. Just as they were ordering dessert, Missy's parents joined them. After showing them the pictures of the office, Cal said that he was going to have her do his office, too. It was becoming quite the business for the little girl.

"Here you go. For helping me out." After handing Missy four hundred dollars, Rosie told her that she wasn't going to be taking it back. "You earned it. I would never have done any of that and would have had people coming by the office thinking that I'd only just moved in. You'd better save it up, too. When we go on vacation together, you'll want to buy shit for the kids. It'll be a blast, too, being able to have souvenirs while away."

Murray was impressed to see Missy asking Cal to hold onto her money for her. He told her that he'd take her to the bank in the morning and set her up an account. After getting dessert, the five of them took a walk around town for a little while and then ended up back at his and Rosie's home. After the other couple left with Missy, he sat on the couch with

Rosie and held her. The two of them were doing that a good deal more now that they'd figured out they simply needed to touch to be in a better mood.

"I found out a bit more magic today. I was on my way to talk to Missy when I realized that I could dress myself. I was thinking that I should have worn a heavier coat when I was suddenly wearing one. Not that I was cold, but it was just chilly enough for—is that the bear in me? That I'm more warm than other people around me?" Murray told her that it more than likely was, as he was chilled all the time. "I noticed that about you bloodsuckers. You seem to be overdressed for everything. I thought it was because you were used to being dressed up, but Hammy is like that even in his own home."

"When we sleep together, I snuggle up to you because you're warm. I never thought of it because of you being a bear." She said that she could also feed herself. "What do you mean? I'm sure that you've been able to feed yourself for a while now, honey?"

"Funny. Smart ass. I can make food appear. Not just snacks, though, that's what I wanted, but a steak too with trimmings. This morning, I even made breakfast for Joey, and he loved it. Did you know that he has a bit of magic, too? Like he can just appear outside when he wants to go out. And he loves the cold weather." He had noticed that about the dog, too. "Oh, before I forget. I found your parents a dog. He's not old enough to be away from his mom yet, but as soon as he is, he's going to be able to be taken to them. He's from the same parents as Joey has. The same mom but not the father. I hope that's all right."

"It's perfect. Did you tell them yet?" She told him that she thought it would be better as a surprise to the two of them. "I know that they'll love him. My sister and brother will be coming to town in a couple of days. They're going to take what they want from the castle before we move into it. We'll have to keep an eye on them. Especially my sister. She can be… well, she thinks that she should be first in everything going on. You're still all right with that, aren't you?"

"I am. Now that we've had Doyle, my faerie going in and updating things like internet and shit, I'm more excited than I was before." Murray, too, was happy for the modern touches. They now had cable as well as more plugs throughout the place, along with electricity and plumbing. He was also happy with the showers and extra bathrooms in the home. It was the little things that made him happy anymore. Since finding his mate, he decided that he was happy for a lot of little things that she brought into his life.

"I was wondering too if you'd decided what you want in the castle? I know that Eleanor, she wants to be called Sissy, is going to go over some of the things that she wants with you. Don't let her bully... never mind. That's not going to happen. Have you talked to my dad about Eleanor and Thomas yet? He said that he was going to make sure that you were aware of what sort of people they are. To be honest with you, I've not spent a lot of time with either of them over the centuries. We met up once in a while, then parted ways. It never occurred to me that it was because they were entitled."

"He and your mom both told me about them. I don't think that your mom realized what sort of people they were until she started talking to me about them. I guess your sister has been in trouble a great deal over the years. As recently as a week ago. Lilith told me in no uncertain terms that I was not to allow her to rile me. I don't know, but I think she realized that I'd not do that about the time that your dad did. They both got a big kick out of seeing me handle them. Your dad is going to have fun with this, he told me. Do you suppose they'd be overly upset if I were to just zap them into next year?" He laughed, knowing on some level that Rosie wasn't kidding either. "Anyway, they're not going to take anything that we've decided that we want. Your dad seems to think that they'll try to talk me into giving the castle to them. That since you're the oldest, we can find other places to live that would suit us better. I don't know what that means, but I'm happy to find out."

"Sissy will try and tell you that you're not a pureblood, so you won't know the meaning of living in an ancestral home." Rosie snorted. Then Joey did. "I love how he does that too. Like he's helping you make some kind of point by echoing your disdain for someone."

"I have no disdain for either of them unless they piss me off. According to your dad, Hamilton said that just being in the same room with Eleanor — there isn't any way that I'm going to call a grown assed woman sissy like she's five or something. Anyway, he said that being in the same room is enough for him to want to take a swipe at her. Physically or mentally."

"Thomas is a blowhard. I do remember that about him. He takes a story, too, that you might have told him about long ago and makes it his own. It's like he was the original person in the storyline. Also, something I just remembered, Thomas doesn't have nearly as much magic as he lets on. I'm so glad that I remembered that. He'll try his best to make you think that he's this all-powerful being when he's not. You have a great deal more magic than he has ever had."

"Good to know." Rosie asked if he was an immortal like they were. "I mean, if it comes down to it, will I be able to save my ass if he gets all shitty with me? I won't go in there with a reason to kill him if he's going to be a lesser vampire than I am."

"I'd have to ask my dad about that, but I'm thinking not. Neither would Eleanor have that bit of magic. She can play around with fire, to make a ball of it while twirling it around, but that's about all she can do with it. Once it leaves her hand, it's nothing more than a burnt-out match." Murray could see that she was filing away this information for later. He had a feeling, however, that it was going to be at the forefront of her mind while dealing with his brother and sister. Murray hadn't seen them in a very long time, so his memories of how they got along were a little fuzzy. He just hoped that they both behaved themselves, or he was going to stand back and watch his mate defend herself.

They were set to arrive around five. He knew that the two of them were close in proximity and friendship. They'd only been born about a hundred years apart. Murray also knew that they would argue violently and then part ways, much like he did with them. Distance and time could make you forget your siblings, but his memories about them were a little bit stronger than theirs, and he wasn't forgetful of some of the shit they'd pulled on him.

"I have a question for you." Murray pulled her closer to him so that he could steal a kiss before she got away from him again. "What happens to the castle and land if your parents move out?"

"You mean permanently? It would go to Hamish if there is no one that wants it. Do you not want to live there? If so, then we would be the ones to oversee the land and castle. If that's not what you mean, then you'll have to explain it to me, love." She told him what she meant. "Oh. No, neither Eleanor nor Thomas can inherit the land in any way, shape, or form. It goes to the oldest. Then to our children. However, if we have no heir, then it would be Hamish, as king of vampires, who would decide who would get it. It might not even be a family member that gets it when he decides. Also, he can take it for himself if there isn't anyone next in line. Did that answer your question?"

"It did. I don't know why, but I have a feeling that you're going to be toast when they get here if we don't do what they want." He stared at her with an open mouth. "I've been doing a little research on my own about the two of them, and they're into some heavy fines with Hamish since way before he took over the king shit. In addition to the fact that they owe some gambling debts that their asses can't cover, they're on the run from a couple of other kisses, that they owe dues to as well. They just can't seem to behave themselves when they're out and about."

He was still sitting in the living room at five thirty when they showed up. Right off the bat, they were arguing with Rosie about whether or not she was his mate or not. Murray didn't bother trying to correct them, either. He knew that Rosie would handle this much better than anyone he knew, including Hamish.

Rubbing his hands together, he decided that he was going to call in the other man. Just so he could have some fun, too. Hell, maybe every one of the others would like to be here when the shit hit the fan. Because Murray had no doubt that it was going to when they tried to control his pretty little mate.

Heading to the kitchen, where Mom was showing off how it had been updated, he heard Thomas whining about how it was a waste of money to have done that. Even after explaining to him — three times — that it didn't cost a thing, he was talking to Dad about their inheritance and how it wasn't going to be much the way that he was spending it all before they got any of it.

Chapter 3

"Dad, can I talk to you privately?" Thomas needed to get away from that woman, or he was going to be in big trouble for killing his brother's mate. He'd do it, too, even if his brother was a bit upset with him about it for a little while. She was too mouthy for his tastes, and he wondered if there was any truth to her telling him that she carried a gun with silver in it. She just wasn't all that nice at all. "There are some things in my...your office that I want to go over with you. I also want to talk to you about some of the things in there that that woman has claimed for herself."

"You'll have to talk to your brother or Rosie. And that's her name, Thomas, Rosie. Not *that woman*. She's taken over the one that I used." He asked his dad why he would allow her to do that. "Well, because she's moved into the castle, son. I've said this to you several times now. Your brother and his mate are moving in here, and your mother and I are going to build us a home not too far—"

"Did she make you move out? It would be just like her to do that. She's a bitch, don't you think?" Dad just stared at him. Then he told him how much he loved her already. "She is hoodwinking you, that's all. I don't like her a bit. Nor does Sissy. That should count for something in her being able to take over our home, don't you think? Murray is blinded by her beauty. And she is that but not a nice person."

"I don't know why that would be something that you'd have to be concerned with, Thomas. Either one of you, as a matter of fact. Murray is going to take over living in the castle, and that's the way it should be. Now, have you gotten your pieces marked?" Thomas said that was what he wanted to talk to him about. "What is it now, son? In the event you didn't notice, we have company around. The king is here, and you're taking up my time talking about something that is of no concern of yours. What did you want to see me about in here? Can't it just wait?" He closed the door quietly behind him so that no one knew where they'd gone.

"No, it can't wait. I need you to lend me some

money, Dad. I have some debts that I've forgotten about that I need to get paid off. I was working with someone on a deal, and they bailed on me and left me holding the bag. A big one at that, too. So now I have to pay the outstanding balance so that I can claim it as my own—"

"The Rosewood project? I do hope you understand that I'm smarter than that if you think that I'm going to put any of my money into that dead project. It is dead too, isn't it? You're lying to me about why you need money." He said that he'd already spent all his capital on things and needed more. "No, Thomas. I'm not going to be giving you any more money. I told you the last time you got in over your head that I'm done funding your little games in life. No more. Just what do you expect your mother and me to live on if you and your sister forever have your hands out for us to put ungodly amounts of money in? We'll have nothing. That's what we'll live on. Now, I'm going back out there to see my king and new daughter-in-law, if you don't mind."

"Dad, I do mind you leaving here without us talking. I don't know where you heard that the Rosewood project is dead, but it's going well." Dad told him that was good and that he didn't need any money. "No. Now you're twisting up my words. I need money, as I said. It might be doing well now, but I'm short on cash for personal things. You don't want me to be seen without, do you?"

"I told him about the project when I got here." He glared at Rosie and told her to mind her own business and that she could just get out of the office. The men were talking. "Oh, but I am minding my own business, Thomas. Your dad asked me to look into a couple of things before you got here, and I did it for the family. Rosewood Production has been out of business for five years now. Putting money into it would be like lending you cash. Your dad would be handing it off to a lost cause. Why don't you tell him the truth? That you owe nearly forty thousand dollars in gambling debts at one casino, and they're not happy you're not paying them. Then there is the hundred grand that you owe some very bad people for killing their daughter when you were only supposed to escort her to a family wedding. There are more things you owe money for, but those two are the top contenders for you getting your ass killed."

"What do you know? Nothing, that's what. Just leave my parents alone, and I won't have to hurt you." She told him that she wasn't afraid of him.

"You should be, bitch. I'm a good deal stronger than you any day of the week."

When he felt himself being lifted from the floor, he tried to pretend it was nothing to him. However, he was afraid of heights, terrified, really. Once his head bounced on the ceiling twice, he yelled for his brother. His humiliation wasn't finished with her seeing how his brother treated him either. His mother and sister saw what he was doing to him as well.

"Put me down, Murray, or so help me, I'm going to kick your ass." Murray told him that it wasn't him that was holding him there. "Sissy, are you doing this?"

"No." Murray told him that it was his mate. Sissy laughed. "No way. There isn't any way that she can do that to him. Christ, she'd nothing but a newbie. Who are you shielding so that you can make her look all-powerful? The butler is doing this, isn't he, Dad? Are you there? Mikey?" Sissy looked around for someone else holding him there, and he glared at the woman.

"It is me. Shall I prove it?" When the bitch waved her arms around, Thomas followed her pattern in the room, barely missing paintings and chairs set up around the room. Each time she came close to the ceiling again, she would make it so he would hit his head. Telling her to let him go, he plummeted to the floor like he was going to crash and be a part of the carpet lying in the oversized room. He was stopped from hitting it in the last few inches. "There, now you're down. But you should be careful, Thomas, about how much you bite off before it comes back and harms you."

"You fucking cunt." Forgetting that his brother was there. Even forgetting that his parents were there too, he lunged at the other woman. Before he could touch her, even to get close enough to put his hands around her throat, he found himself frozen in the air a good five feet from her and his brother holding him around his throat. The part that pissed him off the most was that she didn't flinch. She didn't close her eyes when he went after her. The fucking cunt. "She deserves this, Murray. How on earth can you stand to be around that person? Let me kill her for you, and you and I will have a long talk about getting laid. She lied to me and everyone in this room by trying to make me believe that she held me."

"Tell her that you're sorry." Thomas glared at his brother, telling him he wasn't going to do it. "You apologize to my mate, Thomas, or I will rip your throat out and watch you bleed out. Tell her."

The shake to his body nearly had him sick with pain. There wasn't any way that he was going to tell that cunt that he was sorry. When he was released, Thomas looked at his dad. But he spoke, with laughter in his voice, before he could ask him to defend him. Or, at the very least, take his side in this.

"I'm not going to make her do anything, Thomas. Not that I could, I don't think. Nor am I going to help you out of this situation financially either, as it is your own doing. You deserve whatever you get from your brother on your treatment of his mate. You've been picking at her since you arrived, and there is no cause for it. You were set to attack her, and—" He said he damned well was going to kill her was what he was going to be doing. "You're not helping things. Just tell her that you're sorry for trying to hurt her, and we'll talk about these debts that you owe. You'll notice that I said ones that *you* owe and not we. I have an accounting of the amount you owe, and I'm not going to do it. Not again."

"Dad, what's gotten into you? I'm your son." Dad told him that he and Murray both were his sons, and he was sick of bailing him out. "I suppose you'll help out Sissy? That's not fair, you know. I'm older than her and should be given enough to be out of trouble, don't you think? Then I want to live in this castle too. There is plenty enough room in here for all of us to live. My way, I can keep track of the money that is coming in and out. You never know what sort of spending habits other people have when there is wealth to be had. Oh, and I want to live here too without any kind of fees or dues. Sissy and I are both going to be in big trouble if you don't help us out, Dad, and it will be your fault. You have to help us. It's your duty as our parent. I mean, it's bad enough that you've handed over our birthright to that thing and Murray. Now you're going to be playing—that's it, isn't it? You're playing hardball and showing off in front of Murray and his so-called mate. Well, I caught you, Dad. This isn't funny anymore."

"No." The cunt laughed. Dad turned to her and smiled. It was a smile that made him slightly sick to his stomach. Like she was the best thing that Dad had ever seen and he didn't care who knew it. "You were right in saying that he'd tell me that, Rosie. Right on the nose." Then Dad turned to him. "It's funny how it's my duty to help you out when you're trying your best to drain the coffers. I'm not going to do it, Thomas. Nor for you either, Eleanor."

"It's Sissy, Dad. Are you going senile, Dad? You always used to call me Sissy. Remember?" Sissy laughed and looked at him. "Dad's lost his mind, Thomas. That's all this is. Or, like you said, him showing off. Either way, we're smarter than he is."

"Neither of you are very smart if you ask me. And why on earth would a grown woman want to be called Sissy? It makes you sound like a baby without a nap." Murray kissed the cunt on the mouth and smiled at her as they sat down on the couch. "I'm still waiting on my apology, Thomas. And I will get it."

"Over my dead body, will you be getting an apology from me." Thomas looked at his brother when he just sat there. "She has you pussy whipped, doesn't she big brother? Is this what this is all about? That your little mate wanted to live in the castle, so you kicked Mom and Dad to the curb and have moved in? It's not going to work, just so you know. Whatever plans she's made you a part of, it's not going to work on me."

"I could care less what you think about what is going on. And as for you telling my mate that you're sorry, having you do it or one of us killing you is something that you can count on." Thomas told him to fuck off. "Such language. Not that it matters."

He didn't see his brother move. Nor the cunt. Suddenly, he found himself in his brother's grip, with his beast holding him about five feet from the floor. Seeing Sissy being held in the same way, the cunt looking every bit the old vampire that his brother was, terrified him even more.

Murray was thousands of years older than he and Sissy were. With his eyes a dark blood color, his fangs longer than he'd ever seen on someone before dug deeply into his lip. When he moved his long, silky dark hair back from his cheeks, he could see the pointed ears, so sharp that he was sure that Murray could use them as a weapon, much like his claw-like hands.

Thomas didn't struggle for as much as he wanted to—actually needed to. He didn't even take in a deep breath, afraid that Murray's long nails would tear into his throat. Instead, he tried his best to beg to be let go. It stuck deep in his craw that he was being threatened by his own flesh and blood.

"I'm finished fucking with you, Thomas. Say the words or I will do what is my right. Isn't that right, Hammy?" The king walked into the living room, where they were all in like he'd been there all along. He more than likely had been, Dad and his brother showing off like they were something to the larger older man. Not only that, but the woman with him, a female of equal stature and magic, stood by the cunt. "Launder? Would you be a good friend and make sure that my sister isn't pulling any of her shit and trying to hurt my mate?"

"Oh, she's doing a good job." Thomas watched as the queen hugged both his brother and the cunt. The queen turned to him so suddenly that he jerked away from his brother, causing him to cut a long slit into his neck. The blood there smelled old and sickening to him. The smell of fear was there as well. "Do stop calling my good friend Rosie a *cunt*, Thomas. It's very rude, and I despise that word anyway. Apologize now, Thomas, before I have to get all medieval on you. And I will, too. I'm just about in the mood to do some serious damage to that empty head of yours. Tell her."

The compulsion was so strong that he couldn't have stopped himself from apologizing if he'd had a gun to his head. And with the queen and king in the room, he felt like he did. Once the apology was out of his mouth, his bile coming up from behind the words, he was released. He was not just released but dropped several feet to the floor without a backward glance from his brother as he went to the king and queen.

"I didn't mean it." As soon as the words were out of his mouth, he knew how ridiculous he sounded. He did indeed feel like a five-year-old. There was even a little bit of whininess there as well. "You're going to pay for this. See that you don't?"

"Are you making threats to my good friends, Thomas? Right here in front of me?" Dropping to the floor again, he was baring his neck to the king when he spoke again. "Better, but not nearly enough for the shit that you've caused today. Or even the things that I've been finding out about you in the past. You've been a very…well, you've been giving vampires a bad name. Both you and your sister. Starting tomorrow, you'll find yourself a job and work at it until your debt is paid off. The same with you, Eleanor. The debts that you owe are enormous, and the fines on them are hefty, so I'd find something that pays you well enough to have things like a place to live. You're never to set foot on this land again. Do I make myself clear to the two of you?"

"Yes, your lordship." It burnt his throat to have to say those words to the man. Like acid being poured over an open wound. When Sissy asked where she was going to live, he told her the same, she'd have to find her a job that paid well enough for her to live and pay the debt that she owed.

"I can't do that. I'm not going to find myself a job either. Christ, do you have any idea who I am? I'm not going to do this. You'll have to think of something else. I know. Make Murray pay it. I'm sure that with the castle came all the money that our parents had. Just make him pay it. He should anyway because he's supposed to take care of us. It's his duty." She looked at him, then at the king, as she realized what an excellent plan she'd come up with. "Yes. He needs to get us out of this debt that we're in and make sure that we're never bothered again with anything like this in the future. I don't know why that isn't one of your by-laws. That the children of wealthy families are cared for and housed for the rest of their lives. Yes, I like that so much better. Thomas? What do you think?"

"His duty? Where the hell did you come up with that bullshit? Did you happen to make it up?" The queen looked at him. "I suppose you think the same thing? That your brother has a duty to his family that is too fucking stupid to figure out that you're not owed shit in this world. You do realize that he's a child of a wealthy family as well, don't you? How is his debt paid if you two are the only ones benefiting from the family wealth?"

He sensed a trick there but said that he agreed with his sister. Telling the queen that he really didn't care what his brother did to keep himself clothed and with a roof over his head. It was the very least that he could do was to help them out. He did get the castle, after all. The woman laughed, and it took his breath away at how much it pissed him off to hear her laughter.

"You're just stupid, aren't you?" As soon as the king stood, Thomas realized his mistake, a small one but a mistake all the same. There was no going back on it now. But he needed to try to save himself from being harmed. "Sire, you have to agree with me. She's a female and just not in her right mind."

Thomas lunged again at a woman in this household. As soon as he was close, with only a few inches to go, he reached out his hand to claw the queen's throat out. He'd prove to the king that having a mate, a female, wasn't worthy of the man. As soon as she was dead, then all of them would understand. But it was as if his body stopped, hitting a wall before he could touch the powerful woman.

He felt the air moved over him. His mother screaming had him try and turn toward her. But there wasn't any hope for him to move very much, not with as much pain he was in from hitting the wall or whatever it had been. While he didn't know what had happened, he was sure that the cunt had hurt him. He looked at his mom again.

"Mother?" She stepped back from his hand when he reached for her. "Do you see what you've done to me, Mother? You should have..."

He couldn't make his mouth work any longer. His head felt slippery and heavy for some reason. Thomas giggled a little when he realized how stupid that sounded. When he was suddenly looking up at himself, his head nowhere to be seen, Thomas dropped to the floor. Blood. There was so much blood spilling onto the floor that he was worried that he'd be blamed for the stain.

~*~

Hamilton watched the trees sway back and forth. There were sounds, too, that he could hear. A bird chirping and a cricket making noises, too. Moving enough to get the rocker to move again, he was happy that it didn't take all that much effort to rock.

He didn't think that he had enough strength in his body to make himself breathe if he'd had to.

"Mr. Phelps?" He looked up at Rosie when she said his name. Twice now, she'd been out to the deck, and both times, he'd told her that he was doing just fine. He thought that they both knew that he wasn't, but he smiled at her when she sat down on the ground in front of him. "It was in his head to kill the queen. Thomas thought that with her out of the picture, things would start going his way. Whatever way that was to him."

"I didn't do right by him." She snorted. "I noticed that Joey does that as well. And I even heard Murray do it. You're a bad influence on them. But I'd not have it any other way, I don't think. You don't think that I was a terrible parent to him?"

"No. I don't. He was an idiot if he thought that attacking the queen of your kind was going to get him in any other position than dead and dust. He had thousands of years to figure out that his autocratic way of thinking was going to get him dead. Especially with his attack on Launder. He was a fool." Hamilton said he'd not seen that coming. "I don't think that anyone did but Murray. If he'd not been there beside her, she would have been hurt badly."

"Yes. Though she couldn't have died, she would have been — Thomas has been entitled like he was since he was a child. Maybe that's not the right word to use, not back then, but it's the same principle, I believe. I'd like to put all the blame on his grandparents; they spoiled him something terrible, but I know that I didn't help matters one bit. Lilith said it would come back to bite us in the ass, and it did." She asked him about Eleanor. "Now there is a bitch. My goodness, Rosie, she used to smack the two of us around when she was younger until I just sent her away. That's not good either, but she was so mean to her mother and me. Again, I should have stepped up more, but it's too late for that now." He looked at Rosie. "Did you know that she gave herself that nickname when she was thousands of years old? I never could figure that out. Why a grown woman would be — well, just like you said. She was just too old to be calling herself that childish name. It suited her, I believe. She was a spoiled brat. And now they're both gone."

Hamilton couldn't believe that his children were both dead. Thomas had died at the hand of someone so much stronger than him that it still boggled his mind to think that she'd only been a vampire for a few weeks. While he'd been trying his best to calm his own mate, her hysterics terrifying him for a bit, Eleanor had gone out of the house and to the barn to do the unthinkable. She impaled herself on a rake that had been sticking in a bale of hay for longer than he could remember. She had stuck it in the ground, using her incredible strength so that she could make it work. The only reason they knew what she'd done was that the king had tried his best to save her.

"Is this going to mess things up for you and my son?" Rosie asked him what he meant. "A vampire death in the house. I don't think there are any kind of tales about that, you know, forbidding you from living here, but I want you to know, as far as I'm concerned, nothing has changed for me with the two of you living here." She smiled at him, and he felt the warmth of it all the way to his toes. "You sure know how to make an old man feel good, honey. I was talking to Lilith a few minutes ago, and she's glad to be rid of the castle as well. I think more so now."

"Good to know. I have a faerie, did you know that?" He said that he'd been introduced to him. "He has a lot of friends, and they took a little peek into yours and Lilith's minds and put together a home for the two of you. It's finished."

"Really?" He stood up and then sat down. "We should go and get Lilith to see it with us. Or is she already there?"

"No. I wanted to tell you first. Not that I don't love her to pieces already, but you seem the most affected by what happened earlier. You are, aren't you?" He nodded, then looked away. "I'm so sorry for your loss, Hamilton. I am."

"No. Please don't be. I mean, let me explain something to you first. I'm glad, you see. Not that I'm not heartbroken a bit, but I feel so relieved deep in my heart and soul that I'm frankly ashamed of my feelings." She asked him if he could explain that to her. "I've been thinking about meeting the sun for some time now. Not just myself but Lilith and I have been thinking about it for a while. Some of the things that…well honey, I'm ashamed to tell you, but if we didn't do it on our terms, we knew that the other two would do it for us. And we both felt that it wouldn't be a good ending for us."

"I'm so sorry to hear that." Hamilton leaned back in his chair and stared off into the distance again. "You won't have to worry about that from Murray and I. I'm not saying I won't kick your ass on occasion so that you don't end up dusty sitting in a corner. We're going to have children if we can. Not all from our bodies. I expect and hope that you two will help me out with raising them."

"I don't know why you'd think that, that you'd have no idea how to raise a good child, but we'll be there for the two of you. Forever." She nodded and then stood up. "Are we going to go and see the house now? I find that I'm looking forward to that more and more."

"It's a lovely home. Not at all what I would have thought that you'd enjoy in a home. No stairs at all."

As she talked about the house, Hamilton let his mind wander around. He'd lived here in this area for so long that he could point out things that no historian would ever have been privy to.

He thought about the first time he'd seen a faerie. When the queen of earth had come to see him when his son had been born. Murray had been such a good child. And a better man than he could have imagined. As the two of them walked toward the back of the castle, he pointed out some of the gardens that he would putter around in when he'd been younger.

"You're not what I'd call feeble, Hamilton.

Why would you think that you couldn't still work in the gardens?" He looked at her and wondered the same thing. "I did notice, too, that you had flowers in the front hall when we visited, also around the dining room. When I asked about them, I was told that you were the one who arranged the vases. They were beautiful, too."

"Thank you. So much, child." He did think about how he loved to bring nature into the castle and how much he enjoyed the spring when the blooms first opened up. "I think you're right. I will get my bottom out there and work in the gardens again. It will do me a bit of good, I believe."

After inspecting the house, he and Lilith looked over the gardens. There were plenty of them, too. Something that he wanted to expand on more. After they decided that they were going to enjoy life again, the two of them decided to go on a long cruise. There were so many ways that they could protect themselves nowadays that he wasn't nearly as worried about the trip as he might have been coming across the ocean centuries ago.

Hamilton decided that he was going to do some things with his wife. What was the point of having money if he couldn't use it to have some fun?

Yes, sir, he told himself. He was going to do it. Even if he had to drag her along behind him, kicking and screaming. He doubted that it would come to that, but he was going to have some fun.

Chapter 4

Murray watched Rosie work. There was something so magical about her typing that he had been sitting here for the last hour just being mesmerized by her. He knew each word that she was typing. She'd said each word as she typed it into the computer. Shaking his head, he wondered what she'd say if she told him what he was thinking. More than likely, she'd smack him upside the head and storm off to the other part of the house.

"What do you know about Land Field Airways?" He said that he'd never heard of them. "Yeah, I'm thinking that I've not either. I have an email here that states that I purchased the company several weeks ago, and now they need me to come through on the rest of the funding that I promised them. I think for sure I would have remembered telling someone that

I'd give them more money, don't you? Especially the millions that they're talking about here."

"I know that I would." She handed him a copy of the email. After reading it over, he said he'd get in touch with a friend of his to look into it. "Brad Kirk. I think you've heard me talking about him some with Hamish."

"Yes. I've done some research on him as well. He's a big name in the corporate world, I found out. Also, he's old money. I haven't any idea why people think that is such a big deal. To me, it just means that they've been around a good deal longer and have more than likely murdered off more people to get their money." Murray thought she might be right on that score. Not about Brad but about other people that he knew. "Anyway. I've spoken to him recently. He's going to look into it as soon as he arrives. Which I think is in the next couple of days."

"He arrived two days ago. Hamish told me that he's around here looking for investments. Brad seems to think that there needs to be more businesses around this area if we want to keep people around." She asked him why they'd not had them over or something. "Brad is very…how should I put this? He's very reclusive. He, even being human for all of his life before being gifted immortality by a bear group, he hates them. I think, at one point, he even went on a killing spree. It was justified by the council back then. The ones that he murdered had taken out his entire family line. Including his own wife and children, because he wouldn't allow anyone he didn't know to build on his land. He came home from a trip once to find them all slaughtered and rotting in their own beds. He's never been the same since."

"Poor man." There was a great deal more to the story than he'd told Rosie. And that would be the end of his tale to her unless Brad allowed for her to know more. But Brad had sworn them all to secrecy, and they'd held to that since. "I'll wait for him to come here, but I don't like it. He sounds like a great man from what I've been able to find out about him."

When she buried her head into her work again, he made his way to the darkness. He had come to enjoy his time alone outside and was discovering all kinds of things around the castle that he'd not thought of in decades. He was in the barn, pulling out some of the crates that he'd unearthed when he heard from Marshall.

"I only need a moment of your time." Peering out into the darkness beyond where he was working, he

asked for the older man to come to him. *"I have been injured, my friend. I was wondering if you have anything to wrap up a few wounds for this old man. A good meal, too, if you can spare it."*

"I'd give you everything in the pantry if you needed it, Marshall. Come to me, and we'll go into the castle. We've only just moved in a few days ago, and I might have to do some searching to find something for you." When he came out of the darkness, the scent of his blood made his beast rise up to find the person who dared harm his friend. *"Come. We'll go into the kitchen. My mate is working in another part of the house, so if you don't wish to meet her on this trip, I suggest you keep your howling to yourself."*

"Howling? I've not had a good howl in…well, longer than I can remember, actually. And I would love to meet the woman who was able to tame you. She must be a hell of a mate." He told him that she was all that and more. *"Good. I might need a bit of stitches put in my back."*

Rosie just happened to be in the kitchen when they arrived. She was getting Joey a bone, and when the dog saw the great man, he laid down and bared his throat to the wolf. Petting him seemed to be just what the dog needed, and both man and dog sat on the floor while he cleaned up the wounds that were all along his back.

"You look like someone has beaten you with a whip. I do hope I'm wrong about that." Marshall told Rosie that she wasn't. That he'd gotten into a dispute that had ended badly for both him and the other man. "He'd better be dead, or I'll find him."

Marshall laughed. It was rusty sounding and a bit harsh, his body had forgotten how to produce such a sound, but he hugged Rosie. Telling her that she was a joy to have around.

"You won't think that when you get to know me better. I'm not a nice person. Served in the war and never learned how to keep my opinion to myself and my mouth shut." Marshall only said that he'd not, either. "Good. We might just get along now that you're here. Do the others need to know that you're staying with us? Because you are if you didn't get that memo. You need rest and food. Both of which you'll get plenty of under our care."

"I will take you up on that." Marshall agreeing so readily startled him a bit, but he said nothing. Either he was in more pain than he was letting on, or he needed to lie low. Or it could have been both for as much as he was worried for his longtime friend. "I can sleep in the barn should you wish."

"I do wish that, as a matter of fact. That's where I send all the guests that we have coming along that need several hundred stitches to sew them back together." Rosie hit Marshall on the head and told him that he would be here in the house. "There are a number of beds upstairs that you can choose from. Also, they all have bathtubs should you wish to soak for a little while in one of them."

When she left them to their surgery, he looked at his friend, when he laughed again. Asking him what he was thinking had Marshall laughing all the harder.

"She's a good mate for you, I think." Murray nodded and said that she was the best. "I believe that she'll make sure that you're on your toes, too, for the rest of your days. A good woman like that, she's hard to find."

"You've not met the rest of the women of the kiss. They all have the same temperament and protective style about them. Yet they're all different, too. Rosie is a doctor, and she wasn't kidding about serving. She has a sister who is just as feisty and mouthy when necessary. I don't know if you've met Hammy's mate, but she's the topper in this group.

Scary when necessary and full of it when necessary for that, too. They all are."

Helping his good friend up the stairs, he was worried about him. He was weaker than he'd realized, and once he had him in the bed, he sent the faeries to the kitchen to get him some much-needed nourishment. Just as he figured, Rosie joined the faeries in bringing him food, and he was glad when she decided to look his friend over.

After giving him something for pain, nearly enough to fell a bear, Murray thought, Marshall thanked them both and closed his eyes. It wasn't until they were in their room that she told him what she thought was going on with the other man.

"He seems to have given up. When I asked him about a few other wounds he had on his body, he told me that they were healing, much to his chagrin, and he didn't want me to worry about them." He asked if she was going to do that. "No." She snorted, and he laughed.

"How silly of me to have asked you that. So what are you going to do for him? I'm assuming that he's going to be getting better despite him telling you to not worry with him." She just stared at him. "Right. All right. Tell me what you want me to do, and I'll take care of it on my end."

"Just be his friend." He told her that he could do that easily. "I thought as much. Also, someone is going to have to look into his life. I have a feeling that there is more going on than he's letting on."

"You'll get to the bottom of it, of that I have no doubt." She kissed him on the mouth and got up to go to the bathroom. When she came out, she sat down beside him on the bed and snuggled up to him. She was asleep in no time.

Getting up and then putting her into the bed properly, he wandered downstairs. He wanted to let the others know that Marshall was at his house. Then he decided that if he did that, they'd be there before he could finish telling them. Marshall needed rest, and he wouldn't get it if they were all here worrying about him. Instead, he did a search on his computer with Marshall's name and came up with all kinds of information concerning his good friend. Apparently, he was dead.

Since she already knew that this body wasn't their friend Marshall, Rosie did a more thorough exam on the body than she normally would have. Not that she'd ever cut corners, but she was making sure to check the body over for any kinds of wounds that would have felled a large wolf. It wasn't until Marshall joined her in the large cavernous room that she realized what she might be looking for.

"Drugs. Can you smell them?" Marshall leaned in closer to the body that was on her table and inhaled deeply. He said that he could, but it wasn't a strong smell. "No. I got that, too. Does that mean that it's an old smell or, like you said, just not terribly strong?"

Instead of answering her, he leaned in again and, this time, licked the neck area of the man. She told him that was the grossest thing she'd ever seen him do. As he laughed, Marshall leaned against the table and looked like he was thinking hard about her question.

"Old. Like, I'd say months old. However, what I can taste now is completely different. I taste arsenic. There are also chemicals too. I'm thinking cancer treatment drugs." She asked him if that was something that he'd been needing. "No. Why do you ask?"

"Well, someone wanted this body to be you. His teeth are all smashed in. And the ones that are left aren't enough to run any kind of dental records with. If this person was supposed to be you, can you tell me if chemo would have been in your bloodstream at any time in your life? Or, for that matter, arsenic? They went to a lot of trouble here to make some of the most rookie mistakes I've seen here." He asked her what else she'd noticed. "The body washed up on the shore of a river not far from here. However, there is no river water in his lungs. In fact, he didn't drown at all but was killed by other means. And by that, I mean he was poisoned. Arsenic? More than likely not. I have to wait on the toxicology report to know for sure. But my nose tells me that there isn't enough in this body to have caused death. Also, and this one boggles my mind a bit, what are these marks on the bottom of his feet? Are they something that a wolf shifter has?"

He asked to have a look at them and told her that they were. She studied them harder when he told her that they were horse-shod scars. Rosie told Marshall that she'd not thought to check to see if he was a wolf shifter or not.

"He's not. He's a horse shifter. And I didn't think to check that either until you showed me those." She put the man's feet back on the table and looked at Marshall. "Why did the police or whoever tell you that it was me that you had on your table?

For that matter, why was it in the news reports that it was me?"

Rosie dumped the things out on the table that had come with the body. As the two of them went through the stuff, she pointed out to him how there was just too much information that came with a body from the water. Asking her what she meant had her thinking that what she had was overkill in letting her believe that it was Marshall.

"I have a wallet with a driver's license in it. The picture is of you, but it's either been doctored, or it's a very old picture of you." He said that it was doctored. "Good. All right. There are seventeen credit cards in your 'wallet' that have your name on them. None of the accounts that I've tried are real. I mean, I only checked out the first three, and the account numbers don't work. There is a library card for a library that is no longer in existence. Fourteen cards for points to restaurants all over the United States. Again, they're not associated with any real place. In fact, one of the places that I called has never done point cards."

"What about this?" She took the credit card from Marshall and asked him if he had a card for this company. "No. I've never had a credit card at all. I have cash on me all the time, and the only way that I can lay low is to make sure there isn't a paper trail leading people right to me. But you are right. This does seem to be an overkill of making sure that there is enough physical evidence to mark this body as mine."

He tossed a couple of more things that were in the pile to the side. When he picked up the set of keys, he asked her if she'd been able to locate a car that would go with them.

"There isn't a car in your name anywhere in the world. I'm sure you know that, but I did a deep search even before your supposed body hit my table. All I've been able to find out about you is that you aren't alive as of first thing this morning. You had no credit score. There wasn't any house or car in your name. And as far as I could tell, you've never been born. I don't know how old you are, but you told me once that you were an ancient. Correct?" He nodded. "Then that brings me to this."

She sat down at the computer and put his name in the search bar. She kept pulling up report after report with his name on it. All of them had the same misspelling of his first name, too. Marshall with only one 'l'. She asked him if he had a middle name.

"I don't. Where did they get that letter from?

The 'C' there?" She said that she didn't know. But they had his birthdate wrong as well. He was a man in his early twenties. "So that's made up as well. When did this information start popping up? I'm assuming today."

"After I put in your name the first time, I did print screens of the lack of information. Then, as I was closing down the computer to do the work, it started popping up on just about every website out there. Even a lot of porn sites have your name on them, but they're all fake." He asked her how she knew they were fake. "They all come from the same IP address. Someone is sitting at the same computer putting your name in a lot of locations and doesn't seem to mind who figures out who notices that little bit of information that tells me that it's all fake. Or they don't realize that it can be searched. I even have the address of the place that is doing it."

"Have you been there yet? To the house, I mean?" She told him that Murray was there now, trying his best to figure out why the person was doing this. "Why me? I mean, that's something that I'd like to know too. Like I said, I'm not out there, so why would anyone want to have me pretending to be dead?"

"The kid that is using his computer doesn't know either." Murray appeared in the room and kissed her on the mouth before continuing to speak to Marshall. "He thinks that the man who gave him the thousand dollars to do this is stupid for not thinking of how the IP address was all the same. He'd been the one that changed up the name so that if it came back to bite him in the ass, he'd say that he wasn't using a real person. Also, the kid has a picture of the man on his home security system. Do you know this man?" He laid a good picture of the man standing on a front porch staring right into the camera.

"I do." Marshall sat down and stared at the still picture of the man that had ordered this shit on him. "He's the pack leader. Well, he *was* the leader of the most recent pack that I had contact with. Like just weeks ago. I went there because they were having trouble with their leader and found out that this man, Sherman Tully, was stealing from his own pack. Not just money but goods as well. I let them know what was going on, and he, of course, denied it. It's hard for him to say that the wolf king is calling him a thief. Telling anyone who would listen that it was me that was taking from the pack but they just nod and move on. So, I appointed someone else to the pack to take charge. When I left, I thought things were going well. Now, not only do I find out that I'm dead, but I just found out about an hour ago that the pack has been disbanded, too. That was over three hundred members. Where are they now?"

She could find them. And if not her, she knew that any other member of the kiss could. Reaching out to them, the women, she told them what had happened and what Marshall was looking for. Rosie was so impressed that no one asked about why he was there with them. Instead, it was Lander that got back to her first.

"I can feel their presence. I know saying it that way sounds really creepy, but that's what I feel. There are about what he said, three hundred of them just off the pack ground. Who owns that land?" She asked Marshall, and he said that he did. Then he rented it to the pack. "Well, something is going on. They're on the fringes of what I can only assume is the land. All of them, kids too, are standing around like they've nowhere to go. Also, and I'm not sure why this isn't the first thing I said to you, they seem to be confused and very hungry. How long do you suppose they've been standing there?"

"I don't know. As I said, I was there days ago.

I'm going to go there now. See what I can find out. Also, if you can arrange it, I'd like to have some food and water taken there, too." Rosie said that she'd have it there in fifteen minutes. "Thank you for this. I don't...not that it matters where he is, but is the pack leader I assigned there? I'd like to know if I have to hunt him down for answers." She didn't answer him but just stared at him, trying to gauge how to tell him what she knew. He told her to just tell him.

"Sherman Tully killed him not twenty minutes after you left. Also, the man's family has been destroyed. That's the way he did it, too. He destroyed them. His wife, grandmother, and children were all destroyed by being tossed over a mountainside to hit the stones below. Then, as if that wasn't nearly enough, he had more stones tossed over their bodies by the entire pack to make them complicit in their deaths. Even babies were handed stones to toss to make entire families be a part of it. This man is going to die, you know that, don't you?"

"Yes." She nodded and then stepped away from the computer. "Are you going with me?"

"The entire kiss is. Hamish is pissed and raging about the deaths. Even though they weren't vampires, the land that they tossed the family into was his. He is expecting to get his part in the man's death. His family, by the way, has been supportive of his actions and are right now having a nice party in the open pack land that borders the land that Hamish owns."

Marshall did something that surprised her just then. Standing here the entire time she told him about what had happened, he looked as manic and angry as she'd ever seen a man. But when she said that Hamish wanted his part, he threw back his head and laughed. Like it was the funniest thing he'd ever heard before. Before she could ask him if he was off his meds, he told her to have Hamish meet him at his land now. The big wolf disappeared, and she looked over at Murray.

"What's going on?" Murray asked her if she'd ever seen a pissed-off vampire before. "I'm sure that I have. Why would that be so funny?"

"Because Hammy is the king, and he is the worse kind of vampire to have pissed off at you. Are you coming with me?" She nodded and took his hand. That was when she noticed that the body that she'd been working on was gone as well. She only had to look at Murray for an answer. "Evidence. It might be small to most, but that man wasn't a part of any of the packs around here. As a shifter horse, his family will need to be compensated heavily for his part in the scheme against Sherman Tully. You'll get his body back, but it needs to be there for this."

While she didn't really care if the body was here or there, she did have to make arrangements to have it taken care of. Also, to have his name put on the death certificate. She was told that she'd have that and more before the end of the evening. She figured that Murray would know a great deal more about what was going on than she did, so she was willing to follow along. Before they left her office, however, she made sure to have bottled water and a large order from several fast food restaurants delivered to the crowd of people. It would take them an hour to get the food, but medical supplies as well as help were going to arrive within minutes. Rosie was happy for the friends she had in special places.

They didn't go there so much as they sort of popped there. While not crazy about the way they traveled sometimes, she made sure that she was going to have a talk with Murray about how much she'd be able to carry. Her medical bag was wonderful, but it wouldn't hold nearly enough supplies that she'd need in an emergency like this one. She was so happy for the others being there.

"You'll have all that you need, my lady." She asked Doul what he meant. "You only need to put your hand into your medical bag, and your hand will fill with whatever it is you need. Medical supplies as well as lollipops that you hide in the bottom."

"Those are for the children." He nodded at her, but she saw something there. "If you tell anyone that I have a stash of them in here, I'm going to be highly upset with you."

"I shan't say a word. I have tasted them, the red ones that I know you favor, and they are quite good. I like the purple ones as well." She told him he'd have to try the yellow ones. They tasted like lemon pie. "Oh, I shall then."

As soon as her first patient came to her, she knew it was going to be a long day. These people had been out here for a week if she didn't miss her bet. And the little boy, Jamie, that she was helping, he told her that they were told not to move until they were told or they'd be pushed over the mountain too. Alive.

"Are you saying that the Wilson family was still alive when they were dumped over the side of the mountain?" He nodded, the fear in his eyes making her sick to her belly. "We're going to take care of him. I promise you."

"He said that no one cared what he did because he was that good. My momma is locked up in the cave with the other people." She asked him how many people. "Ten. They're all like my momma. Pretty."

"Hamish? I have a problem." Two seconds after telling him what was going on, he appeared behind the little boy. After getting information on where his momma was with the other pretty women, breedable women, Hamish told her he left. As much as she wanted to go there too, she knew that she needed to be helping the people here more. The mother fucker got off easy as far as she was concerned. There wasn't going to be any way that he'd not be dead soon. She wanted the cock sucker to be able to—

"Doctor Rosie, you're hurting my arm." She looked at Jamie, then leaned down and kissed the bruise that she knew he was going to have from her squeezing him so tight. "It's all right. I was powerful mad, too, when he took my sister and me out of our bed and brought us here. He just loaded us up in a big bus and told us that if we moved one inch, he'd know it and was going to dump us over the mountain. My sister is only four. She would really be hurt if he did that to her."

"Everything is going to be fine, Jamie. I promise." About the time she had sewn up his arm, the food arrived. It not only put the people in a much better frame of mind, but they seemed to be healing a good deal faster as well. Once they were all eating, she went to find Murray. It was time for some action, and she wanted to be as much a part of it as she could.

Chapter 5

Murray knew that his beast was feeding off Hamish's energy. The man was calm-looking. His eyes, an hour ago, were bleeding and were now the normal shade of brown that he had. There was an energy coming off him, hot and almost liquid, that he knew the other vampires were feeling, too. It was only a matter of time before he let go of his beast, and then things would be over.

A vampire could and would lose control of his monster. He'd done it recently when feeding after so long from Rosie. However, this was going to be nothing in comparison. He could have and was held back from killing his mate. Murray, like the others, saw no reason to hold back the big king. Anything and everything that had been told to these people was warranted. More so, too, if you asked Lauder.

Now, that was someone that he was worried a great deal about.

She was much too young a vampire to be holding in the anger that she had. But she was. Just standing next to Hamish, talking to some of the other vampires that had joined them. Her voice was pleasant, her manners just like a very prim and proper queen might be. But he could see the way her eyes sparked, and her fangs, not nearly as long as Hamish's, would stretch a bit longer than necessary. He loved everything about this woman. When she turned and looked at him, Murray bowed and smiled at her. Her heading toward him had him standing up, but he was not entirely comfortable with her just then.

"I'm trying my best to be a good vampire when all I want to do is leave these people, get that man, and tear his throat out." He told her that would just be too fast of a death for the man. "You think I don't know that? I want to make sure that he's immortal so that I can kill him a thousand times."

"You could." She seemed confused by his answer. "Make him immortal. Then kill him over and over." She turned back to the crowd, and he could see her mind working, so he continued. "However, that's not you. Nor would you make a very good impression on the people here."

"They'd be thrilled after the way that he treated them." Murray simply asked her if she was sure that was what they wanted or she wanted. "Both."

He watched her face as she moved over the crowd of people who were still now wrapped in blankets. Holding onto their children for the fear they still had. Some of them were encouraging their young ones to rest. Others had shifted to take care of minor wounds that they'd gotten and were lying about as their wolves to protect their family if need be. A lot of them, the older group, were still warry and keeping an eye out for Sherman.

"They just want to go home and be safe. Some of them haven't had a good meal in months due to his rules." She turned to him. "You knew this."

"No. But I do. I hope anyway I know you well enough that you'd not just kill a man like that." She told him it would make her no better than he was. "Good point." She looked at him then.

"When did you get so smart?" He said that Rosie was rubbing off on him. "Yes, that's a good save. She is a very intelligent woman. But you're more…people smart. No. Not smart. Savvy. You're better around people than she is. Most of us, I think."

"I don't like them any more than she does. However, I have been around longer and am dealing with my dislike of them more. I've become...well, jaded, one could call me. Or just that I don't give a shit how people are, and I don't want to waste my time in getting to know them anymore. Dead? Well, dead is dead, and it matters little if a person learned anything from his death. The result is the same. They're dead and no longer a problem for anyone."

He could see the calmness roll over her. Her thought process about what he was saying started to mean something to her. As she continued to look over the crowd, he saw how she was helping the people there, too. Laughing a little when a group of the elderly got up to pack up their things, she looked at him again, this time with a glint of humor in her eyes.

"I'm sending them home. It matters little to them that they can witness his death, as you said, but more that they're warm, fed, and safe. Your mate, she provided some of that to them, and I want to give them the rest." Murray bowed to her again. "You do that to piss me off, I thought. But it's more than that, isn't it? You actually respect my title."

"I do respect the title that you have, Lander. I do more than most. I've been around long enough to know that it's a title that is hard-earned and well-used by you like none other. However, it is you, the person that I respect the most. The woman behind the title and the magic that goes with it." She asked him if he'd been around when there had been other kings and queens. "I have. Most of them were failures from the start. None of them compassionate. But you? I believe you to be the best. The strongest, too. Also, and you might not believe me in this, it matters little that you weren't born into what you are. You have filled the space with more of everything than any of the others before you. There will be no others after you. Unless you have a child that wishes to follow in your footsteps. Even then, with your training and guidance, it will be you that others will think of as the person that they have loved and trusted the most. Not even Hamish will be able to compare to your reign. You are the reason that he is as well thought of. Because you, my dear friend, make him what he is."

He wasn't sure that she believed him. But she did look happier than she had before. The anger was still there, but it wasn't as all-consuming as it had seemed to him before. When she reached for one of the bottles of water near where he was standing, he handed her a burger as well.

"I've not spent a great deal of time with you, Murray. Rosie, either, for that matter, but I think I'd like to. The two of you have a calming effect on me, like Hammy does. It's good for me, I think." He told her that he didn't know what she was talking about. "I'm sure that you do, but I'll leave it for now. Tomorrow, after this is over, I'd like for the two of you to come to the house. I have some things that I think the two of you will be able to help me with."

After finishing the burger, she tossed the wrapper into the air, and it disappeared. Murray didn't know if he was more impressed with her when all the trash had just disappeared, but he kept an eye on her. He just smiled at her when she told him that she was going home as well. It wouldn't take all of them to kill the man.

"No. But Hammy might need you here." She shook her head and said that he would be fine with him there. "I'm his friend, Lander. I'm nothing more than that."

"I think you underestimate your magic, Murray. I believe that a great many people do that to both you and Rosie. They won't for long, but for now, that's all right." He asked her if she was hexing him. "If you want to call it that. Put out your hand, my friend."

He stared at her extended hand and then looked into her face. She hadn't asked him if he would take her hand but had said for him to. As he did as she said, he could see that his hand was trembling somewhat. Neither of them commented on it.

"You will take what I offer you." He nodded even though it wasn't a question. "Then I give you freely what you deserve. You will share with your mate, and you will both be beyond powerful. And useful. I give it to you now."

He felt his back ache when it met with something solid behind him. Even as he thought she might well have killed him, he could see Rosie coming toward them. Lander, her laughter making light of whatever was going on seemed to not be the least bit afraid of Rosie. Then suddenly, she was with him, the two of them holding onto each other as they ended up in their castle, their bodies together. Rosie cursing, her threats still coming even as he closed his eyes. Whatever Lander had done to the two of them, he had a feeling that it was going to piss Rosie off more than she was right now.

When he woke, the room was bright with light. If he was honest with himself, he wasn't sure if it was bright with light because of the lamps or the windows in the room that hadn't been there before. Sitting up, looking around as he did so, he reached for Rosie to find out where she was. All he could think about at that moment was the safety of Lander, his queen.

"You should be happy that I've been too busy to mess with her. She's been in and out of the tent that I'm in several times over the last several hours." He asked her what they were doing. *"Lander was called out on a case to find a missing family. Four of them came up missing eight days ago, and for whatever reason, they decided to wait that long before calling in professionals. I'm working on the first of the bodies now. The husband to determine the cause of death."*

"Murder?" He got himself into the shower and was just washing his hair when she answered him. *"I'm sorry. What did you just say to me?"*

"I said it has to be murder. The man is some kind of big deal in the corporate world. I'm waiting on something from that friend of yours, Brad, to let us know the man's name. Lander, of course, is being very hush-hushed about this." He asked her if she'd heard from Hamish about

Sherman. *"No. I mean, I'm assuming that he was killed other than that, I don't give a shit. Those people are safe now and seem to be in good spirits. They're having this big outdoors thing next full moon. I don't know anything about it, but it's supposed to be a thank you from Marshall."*

"It's called a howling. And I've been to a couple of them with Marshall. He'll want to award you too if I don't miss my bet in this." He could feel her tension and thought that it was because of what she was doing. Getting dressed, he made his way to the back yard, where he found Joey and his friend working out in the yard. When it occurred to him he hadn't heard from Rosie, he reached her again. *"What's happening? Do you need me there?"*

"I don't want you to think that I'm over…could you come to me, please?" As he reached for Joey's lead, he transferred himself to her. The dog was startled but didn't seem all that fazed by seeing his mistress again. Once the dog seemed to understand whatever was going on, he stood by the doorway to the tent and didn't move.

Rosie was standing over the body of a large naked man. Even from where he was standing, he could tell that he'd been in the water for several days. While waiting for Rosie to finish what she was doing, he looked around the large tent.

There were two computers nearby. A laptop sat on a shelf next to where Rosie was working, and he could hear Hamish and Lander talking to each other on it. The other two computers were on, but he didn't have any idea what they were processing. He continued his search of the room just as Rosie spoke to him.

"There is a man outside this tent that says that he's in charge." She didn't look up from what she was doing but was whispering to him. "I know that he's not. When I agreed to work with Lander, I was told that she would be the only person that I would ever answer to. So I'm not sure what his beef is with not being able to boss me around."

"Is he actually succeeding at it? Because if you tell me that he is, then I won't believe you." She grinned at him as she lifted what he assumed was the liver of the dead man to the scales in front of her. "How is it possible that we can have this conversation with each other and not have it recorded in the mic that is two inches from your head. At least that's what I'm assuming is going on."

"Robin is a wizard at making things work for me." He nodded, then looked around the room again. "I want you to go over to the computer on the left table. That one is also working with magic. All you have to do is put in the name of the man that I'm working on as soon as I say it. I'm still waiting on Brad to — I have it. Can you do that?"

He didn't have a clue what was going on, but he was willing to do whatever she needed. Murray spoke to Hamish when he entered the room, too, and figured out that he wasn't being recorded either. He started to ask him what the hell was going on when he shook his head. Okay, Murray thought, he'd do what he was told until he had a better grip on things.

Telling the computer the name of Stanley Johnson, he watched as it seemed to be bringing up about every article that the name was mentioned in. When it began to slow from the dizzying speed it had started out on, Hamish told him to read off what was there. But to not move around the room anymore than he had to. It was then that Lander came into the room dressed in what looked like a divers outfit.

"Stanley Johnson, forty-one. Never married and had no children. He is the CEO and sole owner of Landfield Airways." He remembered the name from when Rosie had mentioned it to him the other day. They had been asking for money. Rosie, clearing her throat, had him reading on. He read all the things that the man had been up to since graduating from high school at the tender age of nine. There was more, but he stopped when Brad, their friend, was shoved into the room like he'd been held captive not seconds before.

Looking at Hamish, he could see that he wanted him to keep his mouth shut. Brad looked at him and Hamish but didn't acknowledge them in any way. Instead, he turned to the two men who had joined them in the room and told Brad to shut his mouth and to sit down. He didn't have time to move out of the chair when Brad sat on his lap. This was the strangest thing that he'd had going on in a very long—

"Mr. Kirk, I'm only going to ask you this one more time before I put a bullet in your head." The second man put a gun to Lander's head and held Rosie close to him. Again, he was told to stay still and watched as things played out in front of him. "How will you feel if you telling me no again ends up with both these women dunked in the river too?"

~*~

Rosie kept her eyes on Murray. He was doing much better than she thought he might with her and

Lander being held at gunpoint. Not that it bothered her overly much to be held like this, but she knew a great deal more than the man holding them did. Like the men who were at the back of their tent recording everything. Also, that most of the people in the room were immortals. Stupid jackass.

"I'm not sure why you'd think that I care about these women and if they ended up dead or not, but I haven't the slightest idea who either of them are. Other than the vests that they have on, they're just another FBI agent to me. Who, I might add, are people that I'm usually very friendly with." The man with the gun pointed at Lander said that he needed to make the call. "You know, you keep saying that. For me to make the call. What the hell kind of call… do you wish for me to order some pizza? Christ, that sounds good. I've not had a really good cheese pizza in—ladies, do you think you'd like to share some good pizza with me?"

"Call Main Street Pizza. I had some of theirs last night when I arrived. It was hot and spicy…you want a cheese pizza?" Lander looked at her after getting no answer from Brad. "I don't know you all that well, but I'm betting you like one hot and spicy. Like men."

"I don't like pizza all that much. But if they have some subs, I'd love a hunter's sub. In the event that they don't know what that is, it's all the meats and bacon dragged through the garden." She'd had a sub like that with Murray once. It was so thick with turkey, ham, beef, salami, and whatever other kind of meat the place sold doubled up on a long bun with lettuce, tomato, onions, hot peppers, and mushrooms. Her mouth was watering for one now.

"That does sound really good. We can split one if—"

The gun going off had her nearly pulling her own gun out. It must have startled Murray, too, because he'd nearly knocked Brad to the floor. The man had this mischievous look on his face like he'd enjoyed pissing off the man in front of them as he got himself adjusted on Murray's lap again.

"You only had to tell us to shut up. Firing a gun over the body is going to cause this young woman trouble, I'm betting." The gun holders said that she wouldn't be around long enough to complain. "You really have a hard-on for us to all cooperate with you. I'm betting if asked, the women don't have the first clue what you're going on about."

Rosie watched as they both acted clueless.

She'd bet her entire fortune on the fact that not only did they both know what was going on better than the man in front of them, but that the only dead man in the place was going to be the one on the table. Also, if they didn't behave, the two men holding them hostage.

"Rosie, can I ask you questions?" She glanced at Murray but didn't answer him. "I'm assuming that this soon-to-be deadman hasn't the slightest idea what or who you are."

"That's right." He then asked her if he was the reason that she wasn't speaking to them through their link. "I'm not at all good at it yet, and he told us when he brought us in here that he could feel when we did it. I don't think that Lander is having any trouble, but I'm too freaked out to try and get by the man."

"He can't, not anyone in the world—not even Hamish can hear when you and I talk, love. It is formed by the two of us and can never be broken but by death." She looked at Hamish and then back at him. "I promise you, no one can hear us. But for now, this whisper method will work because the man is only human and cannot hear us, but it will work because it's keeping us all informed. You and

I will practice more when we get out of this. We will get out of this, right?"

"Yes." She looked at the computer and then back at her body on the table. "The man with the gun is Wayne Peterson. He killed the man on the table, Stanley Johnson, the big wig. Also, a woman and two children that were at his home at the time, and they were put into the car with him. However, Lander was able to get to the woman and children before they drowned. I don't think she actually got to them in time so much as she was able to save them as they'd been able to escape the car. The water would have been too swift, and she helped them get to someplace safe. I'm not sure about that. Lander told me that they'd been hiding along the water's edge, hoping someone would find them. They're safe with the FBI right now."

She leaned over Johnson and pretended to examine a wound that she'd already noted and knew the cause of. As she thought of the tale she was telling, she made sure to keep her hands busy and her mind alert to things going around her.

"Peterson hasn't any idea who I am. Nor that he sent me the email the other day demanding the money that I was supposed to have promised him.

By the time he did that, not only was Johnson dead, but he'd been frozen—Lander told me—and was waiting on me and now you to get the money to him so that he could flee the country before he had to dispose of the bodies. The woman and children are of no consequence to anything going on only in that they have been held hostage too." Peterson asked her what she was doing. After telling him that she was doing her job, he put the gun to her head. Speaking to the man, she never took her eyes off of him when she could feel the other three men in the room, Hamish, Brad, and Murray stand up. "I haven't any idea what the fuck is going on right now. If I don't do my job, I don't get paid. You've never given me any indication as to what the hell you want with me, and I'm not going to stand around with my thumbs up my ass waiting for you to order pizza, subs, or make whoever that man is over there call someone. If you ask me, you don't have any more ideas about what's happening than I do. Tell him who to call or get off the fucking pot. We're working here."

He pulled back the gun like he was going to use it on her. All she did was let just a little of her new self go, and he backed off. Not sure what he was seeing, she was happy that she didn't have to kill the man. There was still the confession to get and the reason behind all this shit.

"You're very mouthy, aren't you? I might have to take you with me when I get my money." She growled. It had never occurred to her to growl at anyone or anything, but she felt Joey come up behind her and knock her legs. "We'll see how you use that mouth of yours when I have you alone."

When he turned to Brad, she watched Murray. He wasn't nearly as pissed off as she might have thought he would be. But she did worry about Hamish. He looked like he could tear a hole through the man in front of her without a second's hesitation. She might even enjoy that at some other time.

"Brad Kirk. I am going to ask you one more time to call and get me the money that I asked you about." Brad glanced at her and then back at the man. "You were sent an email several days ago telling you to send me thirty million dollars. You purchased an airstrip called Land Field Airways several months ago from Johnson here under your umbrella corporation—I cannot believe that I have to explain this to you. With all that I've heard about your corporate connections, I would have—never mind. I want the money sent to my account now. If you had just done what you were told then, then none of this would have been necessary. Does that explain shit to you enough that you can get off your ass and do it?"

"Land Field?" It was Murray who explained to Brad what had happened before he smiled. "I didn't purchase anything in the way of an airstrip. I have no use for one. If I wish to go someplace, then I just go." He stood up but didn't move when Murray told him to wait. "You have the wrong person."

"Don't be stupid. I've no time for this." Brad shrugged. "It was you. Johnson told me that he sold the airstrip to a man by the name of R. R. Thimble. And after a lot of digging, I found that it's one of your companies. Don't fuck around with me. I need that money now."

"I don't know what to tell you. I don't have a company by the name of Thimble. Nor do I know... well, I think I might know who that is now, but I didn't at the time. I didn't buy the airstrip, nor do I have a company called that. I might have to do some more work on it, but they'd not...Ah yes. They're here. You know, you should do a better job when you're searching for people. You know, like what they might be or how many friends they might have in places around them. It might well have saved you a good deal of time and, well, life had you been a bit smarter."

"What the hell are you talking about. Who's here?" Brad told him that he was friends with some bears. "Sure you are. And I'm the king of Sheba. Get me my money."

"Everyone, please do not move." Rosie watched the sides of the tent as it swayed a bit more than she thought the wind might do to it. Brad moved away from the computer as he put his hand on Joey. "He won't be hurt either, my friend. I'm assuming that you're the R. R. Thimble?"

"My sister and I." There was no more said as the biggest black bear that she'd ever seen came into the tent on his hind legs and his paws with enormous claws at the end of his arms held up like weapons.

Christ, it was scary to see something so close and so huge. Her instinct was to run, but the moment that Murray was standing next to her, she felt calmed in a way that she'd not in a long while. It was a few minutes before she realized that she was no longer in the tent but outside of it, watching the King of Sheba, aka Peterson, being arrested by the FBI while big bears mingled around the site and got into things.

Chapter 6

Murray had never had such a need for his mate. It might have been the growl that she'd turned against Peterson, but he didn't care at the moment. Instead of trying to figure it out or even to think it through, Murray lifted Rosie up onto his lap and tore at her clothing. Even that was taking too long.

He had barely been able to get her to the closest hotel. If not for Hamish laughing and making him aware of where he was with her, he might well have taken her against the closest tree, no matter of the fifty or so people that had been lingering around the site where she'd been working. He had been able to restrain himself long enough to find an empty room and get the two of them in it.

As much as he wanted to free her flesh for him, his need was overwhelming, and he bit her through the lacey clothing she had on, and blood, rich and hot, spurted into his demanding mouth. He pulled hard and drew a mouth full of her blood into his and felt her healing essences begin to fill him. Pulling her hips forward, he began to move her over his cock as he suckled, rocking them both into a heated frenzy. Her arousal poured into him, her scent stronger because of it.

Letting go of her breast, he unsnapped the front closure, and her amble breast filled his hand, and he licked the wound closed that was there. He didn't know where it had come from; it didn't matter, but she was healed now, and he was glad for it. Taking another swipe at the creamy flesh, he helped her stand and began pulling at her pants. He wanted her, to taste her, to bring her to climax right now.

Her pants were down around her knees when he buried his face between her thighs, her clit already swollen with need and peeking out of her nether lips just for him. He pulled the tiny nubbin into his mouth and nipped at it, then laved the tiny wound with his tongue. Spreading her wide with his hands, he ran his fingers up between her legs and slowly pushed two fingers into her heat even as he ate at her.

Moving to the edge of his chair in the room,

Murray moved onto the floor and turned her around so that she could sit down. As soon as her ass hit the cushion, he pulled her forward and licked her in earnest, devouring her like she was his last meal. His fingers fucked her quickly now, in and out, stretching her for him. When she began to beg, wanting him to finish her, he reached down with his free hand and began to unbutton his pants and free his cock. It sprang forward and seemly reached for her heat. Wrapping his hand around his shaft, he began pumping himself, waiting and ready for her release so that he could enter her.

Murray knew that if he slammed into her at the beginning of her climax, she would be tight and wet. And from his little experience with her, he knew that she would peak again before he found his own release within her heat. When Rosie stiffened, then tightened around his fingers, he knew that she was close, and when she bowed up and screamed out his name, he pulled her off the chair and onto his cock, slamming hard into her. As she bowed back against the seat again, baring her throat, he brought her forward toward him and bit her just as she sank her own teeth into him. He roared his own release around her throat, his cum filling her the way her blood did him.

When she settled around him, spent, he licked the tiny wound closed and held her to him for long moments before he laid them both on the floor. Not releasing her, he reached over him and pulled the seat cushion off the chair and settled it under his head, and he pulled her over his chest.

"That was down and dirty. I don't think you've shown me that side before." He could barely move, much less answer her, so he nuzzled her neck and spooned in behind her. "Don't get too comfy, buddy. This floor is hard, and I don't want to be found here in the morning by the staff."

With a bit of his magic, they were in their bedroom. Rosie was awake when he pulled the blankets up and over them. Closing his eyes, he decided that he was just too tired and sated to make such a fuss about her not being as sated as he was at the moment.

Waking, he found himself not just alone in the bed but in the room and house as well. Sitting up, he reached as far beyond himself as he needed to find Rosie with her sister in Ohio. The two of them had been talking for a while so without making himself a bother, he went to the shower to get cleaned up.

He'd talk to her later. Now, he just wanted to find out what the hell had happened that had gotten Brad and Hamish tangled up in the web of Peterson.

It was Brad that he met first. After giving him a big hug, the two of them sat in the living room of Hammy's home to catch up while Hamish finished up with a phone call. It wasn't nearly as twisted as he'd believed but just the mind of an idiot human who thought he was much smarter than he really was.

"All in all, it turned out great. I've been chasing the company called Thimble for a few decades as a matter of fact. The moment that your lovely mate told me that it was hers and her sisters, I knew that I was going to have to invest in some of the things that they have going. I don't know if you're aware of this or not, but you have some pretty savvy people in your family." Murray told him that he did indeed know that. "Of course you do. Where is the lovely mate anyway? I thought for sure once you people found your mates, you were inseparable or in bed together fucking each other's brains out all the time. Don't tell me that's not true. It will sadden me for the rest of my days."

"We've not been together long. But we do fuck

when we can. Don't tell your future mate that, Brad, you're going to be fucked up if you do." That was all he could tell the man before Hamish came into the room with Lander in his arms. "These two, however, make up for any of the rest of us finding a nice quiet place for a good fucking. They're forever at each other."

The four of them settled in, and when Rosie joined them, she sat down on the floor in front of him. Not sure why she'd think that was a good place, but he picked her up and put her onto his lap, and held her there. He could almost taste her happiness.

"What's going on? I'm glad that you're happy, but you've not been with me, so I know that I've not made you squeal with laughter yet." She turned and looked at him, then smiled. "You're the most beautiful creature that I've ever had the pleasure of being in love with, Rosie Phelps."

"And I love you. Ruby is going to have a baby." They all celebrated, and he reached out to his sister and told her how happy he was for her. "She just found out. After going to the sleuth doctor, she wanted me to be the first to know. It wasn't until later that Calhoun told me that he'd known for days, but it made her so happy to tell me. I'm so excited for them both I could bust."

The rest of the evening was spent with the rest of them talking about upcoming meetings that Hamish and he were attending. It wasn't until Brad left them that he had a lot of work that he said he needed to get finished up that he was able to talk to Hamish and Lander about the magic that he and his mate had gotten.

"It wasn't my magic that I gave you. I was only the holder for it." Murray looked at Hamish and then back at Lander. "Several days ago, I was approached by your parents. They asked me if I would help them out with the distribution of something. I had no idea what it might have been, but I told them that it would be my pleasure to help them. It wasn't until after the death of your brother and sister, more than well-deserved if you ask me, as we're finding out that I figured out that the magic they had should have been yours in the first place. I'm still working on details, but I have about all of it gathered for you both now. First of all, I want to tell you about Eleanor."

"Wait. I'm sorry. My parents asked you this before they were killed. Do you think they…I won't believe you if you tell me that they knew what kind of people they were before they were ordered to death." Lander told them that they had not. "Good. Then what would she come to—"

"If you would just shut the fuck up, I'll be able to tell you. Christ. Why did I think this would be easy?" Murray looked at Lander when she stood up and began to pace. "She had an idea once she started talking to Rosie. Not that Rosie had told her anything about them, but it was her actions and her manner. She'd, your mother Lilith, hadn't been around a lot of mated people. Much less people her children's age. So she, sadly, thought that they all pretty much acted like they did. Entitled little fuckers." Rosie cleared her throat. Lander sat down hard.

"You're mucking this up. Just tell him the facts." Murray asked if she knew that if Rosie had been told something, he'd not. "No. I know nothing. Other than the fact that she's going around the bushes, upside the castle, then around the state before coming to the fucking point. Just tell him and me what you know, and we can move on."

"Fine. Elenora killed a great many people before she'd become a full vampire. The list of names and ages is astronomical. Not only that, but some of the names on the list that came to us were beings that were there to protect your family. Faeries and

Brownies. There were unicorns, which I didn't know about, as well as other creatures too. The queen of the faeries, someone that I had only just met, came to me when I was going over the list. I was saying the names, like under my breath, and I guess I finally said one correctly. That brought her to me. She was pissy with me until…well, she won't do that again."

"I might." Both he and Hamish went to the floor. It mattered little what titles anyone around this woman carried; she was the queen of magic, and she could kill them like no one else could. "Get up. Damn it, Lander, you told me that you'd do this correctly. I have to agree with Rosie here. You sort of get around the bushes, don't you? Hello, Rosie. My goodness, you are more beautiful than I remember."

"Hello, Sarah." He didn't know what to think when his mate embraced the queen. When they were both seated, Rosie dragged him up from the floor and told him to sit. The queen stared at him while Rosie introduced him to her. "Sarah, this is my mate, Murray Phelps. I know you know his parents."

"You didn't tell me that you knew her." Rosie told Lander that she'd not asked. "That seems to be something that you'd mention to someone when you're becoming friends."

"All right. Lander, this is my godmother Sarah, queen of the magic. She isn't my sister's godmother, but her sister is. The queen of faeries, Allison. We've known each other, I guess, since I was just a kid." Murray watched Lander as she seemed to have no idea how to continue. It was Hamish who asked how it had happened. Then it was Sarah who said that she wanted to tell the story. "All right, but no embellishments. I want to go home and have something to eat, then I want to fuck my mate. Hurry it along, or you're going to be telling it to an empty room."

Murray was shocked, but he also thought it was funny. Sarah, a being that he'd never met before, seemed to take it in stride that Rosie could be and was a bitch to her. As soon as some food, a lot of food appeared in the room, he watched as Rosie and Lander both filled plates up of pizza and chips before sitting back down.

"I was actually trapped in a snare when I first met Rosie. She was nothing more than an infant. Her playpen, I believe what her parents had put her in, was sitting out under the tree that I had been snared in. The day was so beautiful. I had never dreamed that it would turn out the way that it did. I so love the sun streaming in the trees, and that's what alerted me to know that I was needed. I was trying to free some of my little creatures when this beautiful little girl with the most beautiful eyes just looked up at me and smiled. She untangled me of the netting and then—" Rosie told her that she'd been sleeping and to stop making her out to be something more. "All right. Rosie was in the yard with one of those terrible creatures that come along only once in a while. It was a troll. A young one that had captured me, and he was ready to drag me to his home for his supper when Rosie came tumbling toward me with a large stick." She looked at Rosie. "Is that naked enough for you? The story is so much better when it has color in it, you know. Every author knows that."

"No one cares what the day was like. Nor do they care how old I was when I was helping you. If I had known then what I know now, I might well have left you there all tangled up." They both snorted, and Murray had to laugh. It was Hamish who said he might like the colorful version sometime. "Don't suck up to her. She's too friendly, and that's what got her wrapped up when she should have been home mending flowers or whatever the hell you do."

"Thank you, Hamish. Anyway. She was just

a child when she really did save me. If not for her slapping the troll around, he would have hurt us both. As it was, while she had him distracted, her sister, Ruby, a much nicer person than this one, wouldn't have been able to get me untangled. After that, Allison and I both swore that we'd care for each of the girls until such time as they told us they no longer needed us." Sarah looked so sad. "It was just after their parents died that they both came to us and said the words that would…they called it freed us from their care, but it wasn't freedom that they gave us but a good deal of sadness."

"You were too busy to be messing around with a couple of kids. Besides, I'm sure you remember coming back to help me a few times after being told that you were free of us." Sarah gave Rosie the most impish smile then. "She saved my life a few times as well. And no matter how many times I let her know this, she seems to think that she still owes me her life."

"You saved her when she was in the service." Sarah nodded at him and then told him the other times, all at times of great need from Rosie, that she'd been there for her before. "I knew that she was hurting from depression, but I never knew that she had been able to go that far."

"No one does." Sarah agreed with his mate. "She kept showing up. Just when I could see the light fading from…it matters very little now, to be honest. I couldn't be happier with the outcome of her saving me. Without her help and intervention, I'd not know what it's like to be loved by my mate."

When the two of them hugged again, Murray saw something that he'd not noticed before about his mate. Standing up when they were still hugging, he put his hand on Rosie's back and then slid his hand up to under her hairline. The scar there had him staggering back.

"That wasn't an attempt." He nodded, still holding onto the couch, when he realized that the scar had been the removal of her head. That at some point in her life, an attempt had been made to kill her by removing her head. "Sarah, catch him."

When he opened his eyes, he was in a room that he didn't know. Not that it mattered. The bed was secondary to the room he was in. Sitting up, careful of not making himself sick, he moved his legs to the side of the bed and held tightly onto the mattress.

"Your lordship." He knew what a faerie was; he had one of his own, but this creature was larger than his and was walking around the room like a normal person would. "I'd like to think that I'm a normal person."

"I'm sorry." She sat down, and he could tell, too, that she was doing that for his sanity. "Where is Rosie? I don't know that I'm ready to know where I am yet, but if you could tell me where I might find my mate, I think I would feel better."

"You're doing very well, but she is in the yard." He asked her if she was all right. "She is. More than all right, my lordship."

"Okay, you've called me that twice now. I don't know where you might have gotten the idea—why do I suddenly have all this information in my head?" She, her name was Jam, told him that he'd relaxed enough to find it. "I don't understand. It's okay, but I don't understand."

"Lady Rosie is coming along now. Her sister Ruby is with her. Lord Calhoun is coming as well, but he'll be along later. He is his great bear." Nodding so he'd not have to speak. He wasn't entirely sure what would spill from his lips. "You will be all right, my lord. I promise you."

He didn't move once Jam disappeared. Standing up, he made his way to the doorless opening and stood there watching what his mind did not want to comprehend. It wasn't until Rosie wrapped her arms from behind him that he felt a little calmer. Putting his hands over hers brought him more relief.

"I told Sarah to take you home, and she thought it was funny that I wasn't more specific. So she brought you here. You had a big bump on your head; it's healed now, and I was actually grateful for her magic to keep you from bleeding more than you did. Are you all right?"

"I keep being told that I am." He turned in her arms. "I'm better with you here. I was...I have no idea what I was thinking before you came in. Some things about my sister and brother. That they'd been responsible for a great many deaths than anyone had thought. All these details are just there for me to read or think about. Is that normal?"

"I'm not sure what a normal thought would be for you after today." He laughed and decided that he sounded a bit manic, so he stopped. "I haven't had anything to do with this realm, Sarah or Allison, since I got out of the service. I know that she's always been in the back of my mind, but I never called on her."

"Do you have magic?" She said that she was

gifted with the ability to remember things that she read. "That's why you were able to be a doctor at such a young age. There is more, too, correct?"

"No. At least, that's what I told them. Ruby, too, was given a gift. Hers was the ability to do the same, but instead of being a surgeon, Ruby chose to be a doctor of the mind. It was to keep us... I guess you could call it safe from whatever happened around us. We still got sick and still would have died — In fact, Ruby was set to die before we came here. She had cancer throughout her entire body, mostly in her brain, some that even the doctors hadn't found yet. We could have called on them, I guess, to heal us, but that's not what we asked for when we helped the two of them."

"You had more to do with Thomas and Eleanor than you let on, didn't you?" She nodded, then shook her head. "One of the women told you then. Gave you some kind of heads up and you looked into it."

"Yes. Well, sort of. She gave the information to Ruby, and she gave it to me. Are you upset with the information?" Murray thought about how much information that he did have on them and held her tightly while some of the information came to him in the form of video. He could see every single nasty deed that they did. And he wondered why he'd not noticed what they'd been up to. "You didn't notice because you didn't spend a great deal of time with them. The sad part is, I think your mother was a victim of theirs for a lot longer than anyone thinks."

"The castle." He didn't know if she was just giving him what she thought he could handle or not, but he was all right with her answer. "We'll head home tomorrow. Some things are going on around here that need some attention. Nothing bad. I just didn't know how long you were going to be out, so I said that I'd help. Ruby is here, too. When Allison showed up at our home, Ruby was notified. Sort of like a radar thing. You are all right, aren't you, Murray?"

"I believe that I am." She took him into the yard, and the things that he'd been looking at earlier didn't seem to tax his mind this time. There were unicorns, a creature that he'd only heard of before playing in the yard with what he thought was a griffin child. There were other creatures as well, dragons and camels, and he watched two buffalo in a larger field enjoy the sunshine. He was careful to keep his hand in Rosie's while they were there. There was no point in pushing his luck. Nor his sanity.

"You're tense." He told her that he was just getting his mind to center. "All right. If you say so. Me having Sarah and her sister in my life, it doesn't freak you out, does it?" His laughter spilled out, and he didn't catch it in time. "I see. I don't, but I suppose that it was smart of me not to tell you everything. Even though I shared my memories with you, you still seem sort of…I don't know, Murray, freaked out about all this."

"You did share your memories. I guess you could say that I didn't want to dig too deeply into those. I was more focused on making new ones with you." She nodded and sat down on the bench that was in a large tree-lined area. Murray sat down next to her. "This is, all of this is a bit more than I think I would have thought you'd had in your memories. You never gave me any indication that you had any magic. I guess your touching and blasting a few people when you touched them is explainable now. Not that it matters. It's all what you are. The woman that I love. But you have to admit, this land and the things going on around here are a bit more than normal."

"Yes, I can see that. I've only been here a couple of times." She looked at him before speaking again.

"My head had been removed when—" He put his hand over her mouth.

"I can't. Not yet. I know that it was horrific. I can see the scar and know that. But also, you're here. Now, with me today. That's all I want to see and think about." She nodded and smiled at him. "Someday, I might want the story. At this time, I can't think of a time when I would want to hear how it happened to you or who might have done it, but as I said, you're here, now with me, and that's more than I ever hoped for in my lifetime."

"I can live with that." Rosie leaned her head on his shoulder as the two of them sat there talking about the little things going on around them. When a faerie came to see them, he wasn't sure that he wanted to be bothered by anyone yet. His time with his mate, now more than ever, was something that he didn't want to share. "I have to go. Lander is working on something, and I promised her that I'd help. You can hang out here if you want. Or come with me. It's entirely up to you."

"I want to be where you are." He needed to be close, and when she stood, so did he. In less time than he thought it took him to blink, they were both standing in their living room. Disappointment washed over him. He was already missing the other realm so much.

He did end up going with Rosie. She wasn't out in the field like he had assumed she'd be but rather helping Lander with some death certificates that had been given to her in the name of being gone over. Murray did know a little about what Lander was looking for, but some of the certificates were decades old. Finding Hamish in his office, he joined him there when he kept getting in the way of the other two.

"Run you off, did they?" He nodded and sat down. "You lasted longer than I did. I was in there helping Lander last night when she chased after me with a gun, scared ten years off my life. Of course, my sister thought it was hilarious, so I left with my tail between my legs, so to speak. Having magic has certainly made my job a good deal better than I thought it would be. And Robin, having worked with the council for all those years, has given me an insight into things that I never thought to have. Those other three that were running things certainly had it set up to make them wealthy."

"I heard about that. Robin worked for them in some way, right?" Hamish explained. "All right. That I didn't know. So, she was a slave for them. I'm glad that you guys were able to save her. She and Warren are the perfect couple, it seems like to me."

Murray thought about some of the things that he'd just learned about his own mate and didn't know if he wanted to or, for that matter, was up to sharing them with anyone just yet. When he looked over at his best friend for centuries, he was looking at him as if he was waiting to spill the beans about some trouble he was having.

"I have a lot on my mind. But I did want to talk to you about one thing. My parents. I have...I was given a lot of information about my sister and brother. A lot more than I think you might even be aware of. Anyway, Rosie said that she thinks—however, now that I think about it, she might well know that my mom especially was abused by them. I didn't ask yet. I'm in overwhelmed mode if you want to know the truth. Can you tell me if there is a lot of abuse or something that I might be able...hell Hamish. I don't know what I want to know about this. I don't want to think about my mom being hurt, mentally or physically. But did it come out when you were taking care of them? Did it come out that they'd been hurting her?"

"Yes." Murray felt like his heart had been

stabbed. Not only that, but he felt all his love for his mom come to the surface all at one time, and it had him blubbering again. Telling Hamish what he was feeling, how he wanted to find them again and make them pay, he laid his head on his shoulder when he pulled him from the chair and asked him to tell him. They were both seated in the chairs when Hamish nodded.

For the next three hours, the two of them talked. It hurt him in ways that he hadn't in a very long time to think about how much he had really missed at his home. His mom and dad, too, at a lesser expense of pain, had suffered terribly. He also found out that they had wanted out of the castle because of the memories; very few of them were good to start fresh.

"I was thinking that I wish they had told me, but I can also understand why they didn't, too. I mean, after they were born, I left home and, for the most part, didn't return. However, when I think about all the calls that I missed from them, and times they wanted me to come home for a visit, I wish I would have made more of an effort." Hamish told him there was no point in looking behind. "I know. I should have been paying more attention, too. At the very least, I should have visited them more."

"I wish that as well. Especially having my sister around all the time. I realize with her, I missed a great deal as well. More than I would have thought possible." Murray thought about the castle that his parents had lived in. "Whatever you're thinking, you need to let it sit for a bit before acting on it."

"I was thinking about the castle and home that Rosie and I are living in. It's wonderful, don't get me wrong, but I'm having a hard time getting my mom and dad to come over for visits. I know why now, but I don't want that to keep them from coming over when we have kids. And I think that it will. What would you do?" Hamish laughed. It was full of humor and fun. "You would tear it down, wouldn't you?"

"I'd do what the town wanted. Turn it into a tourist trap, sell tickets, and reap the money. Live on the land or not. I wouldn't, but then that's me. But you can do either. There is certainly enough land there for you to do what you wanted." Murray asked about the money. "Do you need it? I mean, really? Do you need to sell it for the cash? Or, for that matter, for the price of a ticket. Turn the money over to the city for improvements. Make sure that they're being done, and wash your hands of it all. I mean, keep it around. That's your home, but for now, until you're in a better frame of mind and your parents are, let someone else take over its care. Move closer to us, and we'll have fun as a kiss together."

He'd have to talk it over with Rosie, but he liked the idea of not doing anything with it for the time being. Murray decided too that he was going to move his parents closer to where he and Rosie ended up so that they could make better memories and, like Hamish said, wash his hands of the place for the time being.

Chapter 7

"I'm here to deliver an order from the dairy warehouse. It's from Miller Farms." Dill handed over the paperwork to the man at the guardhouse. When he asked for her name and identification, she handed it over as well. Since she'd been doing this particular delivery for about five years now, she had all her things ready to hand over when asked. "I'm supposed to be here by noon, and it's just shy of that."

"They told me that you were coming in early for this one. I'm to tell you thanks and to give this to you." She was handed an envelope along with a gift card from the restaurant. "Mr. Kirk, he's in the warehouse right now and said to make sure that you get some food for you for coming in four hours early. We all appreciate it."

Dill put the card and the envelope over her

visor and went to the dock door, she was told. Not a bad deal for getting on the road a few hours early, she thought. After backing into the space, she was getting ready to get out when her cell phone rang. She wouldn't do two things at once. It was difficult enough to get a trailer backed into a small space and then get the wheels locked and everything without being distracted. Answering the phone with her last name, she sat in the cab.

"Ms. Dillard." She said that it was her and that she wasn't going to be taking a long call to get to the point. "I like that. Right to the point. It's Brad Kirk. I wanted to personally thank you for today. You've saved our butts here."

"Like I told the guy out front, I had time, and I didn't mind. But Mr. Kirk, I can't get this ready for unloading while jawing around on the phone with you." She looked in the cab and saw that her son was awake now. "Is there anything else?" His laughter made her pissy, and she didn't know why.

"No. Nothing else. Go on. Get your work done. I'll talk to you later." She closed the connection and turned to Toby. He was getting his shorts on just as she was opening the door. Dill wondered what he thought they'd have to talk about but let it go. People said all kinds of weird things.

"Don't get out until I tell you." He said 'yes, mom' like he'd heard her say the same thing a hundred times. He probably had. Toby and her had been riding the roads since he was four weeks old, and her fresh out of trucking school. "Don't eat much. They gave me a gift card for the place. I know you've been wanting to try it."

It took her nearly an hour to get her trailer locked and ready for unloading. The man on duty at the doors told her that it wouldn't be long, but he'd have her trailer pulled into the lot if she wanted to get some food. Glad for that, she told him where she was going to be. After getting her gear and her son, they were headed to the parking lot to see if there was room for the big rig.

They had been seated when she remembered the envelope. Stuffing it deeper into her backpack, she was talking to Toby about the menu when they both decided on the big brunch that was going on today. If they could stuff themselves enough, she knew that they'd not have to stop again until dinner. That was fine by her. She hated snacking on the road.

They were in line when she heard from the warehouse. Her load was emptied, and her trailer was in the lot. Glad for the knowledge that she'd be able to get out sooner than planned all the way around, Dill watched Toby fill his plate with two slices of pizza, three burgers, a large load of fries, as well as mashed potatoes, gravy, and fried chicken.

"You do know that we'll eat again, right?" Dill got a salad, something that she sorely missed while being on the road all the time. Toby got himself two glasses of milk and headed to their table. She'd bet her next check he'd be ready for another round of food by the time she got there.

Since it was so early in the day, the place was practically empty. When seated, they put her and Toby in one of the larger rooms alone, and she was glad for that. No one would be so close that she'd feel closed in. It was a problem that she had with larger restaurants. Especially ones with buffets. The room they'd been seated in was devoid of anyone but her and Toby.

"Ms. Kirk?" Dill glanced at the man standing not a foot from her while she was putting croutons on her salad. "You've been difficult to find."

"My name is Becka Dillard. I don't know who you're looking for, but it's not me." He just laughed at her. Finishing up her salad, she turned and left the man there. She was just reaching out to her son when another man stepped in front of her. *"Toby, I want you to find a waitress and tell them that I'm in trouble here. That someone is looking for a woman by the name of Kirk and thinks it's me."*

She could see her son now, and when he nodded, wiped his mouth off, and stood up, she could have kissed him. As he made his way away from the table, she sat her plate down across from her son's and sat down, much to the anger of the two men.

"Ms. Kirk, you're not making this easy on yourself. We only want to talk." She told them that she had an ID and that she'd show it to them if they would just leave her alone. "I have ID too. It don't tell you shit about who I am. We just want to talk to you and then to your husband."

"I'm not married either." She slowly pulled her backpack to her front and slowly eased the zipper down. "I'm a self-employed driver. I don't have a spouse, nor do I have a company that I work for. You're making a mistake, and I'm only going to tell you one more time that I'm not who you're looking for."

"Bradley boy is going to make sure that we're

paid this time." She told the second man that she was happy for him. Then, a gun appeared on the table, and she could feel one ramming into her ribs from behind. "You pull out anything other than a little bitty purse, and I'm going to blow your head off."

She shot the second man before he could wipe the fucking grin off his face. Her gun was pointed at the first guy's head. Really, she was pressing it into his forehead when someone cleared their throat from behind her. She didn't move but told whoever it was the same thing that she'd told the two men.

"I was in line when they approached me. The second one there, he threatened me. I don't take well to that. This guy, he said something about Bradley boy paying him. I just want to enjoy my first good meal in a long time with my son." She could smell Toby. "Are you all right, son?"

"Yes, ma'am. This man is going to help us. He was at the cash register when I got there. He said that you know him." She didn't so much as take her eyes off the man in front of her. "See, I told you that she'd not care. Mom will kill this other man, too, if he don't put that gun down. She's not one to mess with."

"Toby." He said he was sorry, moved across from her, and resumed eating. "Really? You're going to enjoy your food now?"

"I might not be able to if you splatter that man's head all over me. This is the best fried chicken since your grannies. And you know how much I like that." He was calming her. Something that he did very well. *"Mom? Do you know Mr. Kirk?"*

"No." She heard the scrape of a chair and glanced at the man who sat next to her son. "You touch him, and I'll tear you apart."

"No one will bother him. On this, you have my word." Dill snorted at the man. "Someone else I know does that when she's disbelieving of something. You'd like her, I think."

"Doubtful. I don't suppose you've called the police, have you?" He said that he had, and when Toby offered him a piece of his chicken, she glared at the two of them. "This isn't a social event, young man. Eat so that we can get out of here when the police arrive."

"Since my mom is really busy right now, my name is Toby Dillard. I'm sixteen, and she's my mom, Becka Dillard. Not Rebecca, but just plain Becka." Mr. Kirk told him who he was. "Good to know. You might not care right at the moment but she's not really my mom but my aunt. My mom died when someone from another group decided that they'd do a better job than my dad and mom did and killed them off. If not for visiting my aunt, I might well have—"

"Toby, what are you doing?" He told her. She looked at the man for the first time. "Oh. I don't know anything about...please keep the information to a minimum if you don't mind. I don't care if he smells like home to you."

"Yes, ma'am." She watched her handsome nephew stand up and smile at her. "Since you have things under control, and I don't know when we might get to have a meal like this again, I'm going to go and get some more food. Just...if you'd not mind, Mom, please don't make more of a mess with this other guy's brains until I get done eating. All right."

"I want you to know, young man, that I'm going to beat you senseless when we get out of this mess." As he walked by her, he kissed her on the top of her head, and she felt her eyes fill with tears. "That isn't buying you any points."

"Yes, ma'am, I know that. I'll be back." She glanced again at the man sitting there by where Toby had been.

"The police have pulled up and are now in the front of the restaurant. I want to thank you for not making it known throughout the place what's going on back here. This man," she watched the man she was holding the gun on head wobble when Mr. Kirk hit him, "He's going to jail for a long time. He is the reason, along with his buddy there on the floor, why we needed you to bring in our delivery earlier."

"I don't know them. But that man threatened me." He said that he knew that too. The police came, and she felt the bite of a gun put to the back of her head. "I have a license to carry, and that man—"

"Officer Hill, I want you to remove the gun from her head. I told the dispatcher when I called them that I had this under control. Remove your gun, or I will. And you know me well enough to understand that I'm not a man that likes to repeat myself." The gun pressure disappeared. Before she could ask what the hell was going on, Mr. Kirk began speaking again. "These are the two men that were on camera yesterday breaking into the back of the dairy area and pissing into the vats. My staff here worked through the night to get them serialized and ready for today's milk. I also told you that they'd be back and that they'd all but told us that they would. And today, not only did they show up, but they brought a gun into a very public place and threatened my patrons. Going so far as to make it so that one of my very loyal patrons had to kill one of them because you couldn't get up off your fat ass and make sure that the other people here were safe too." When Kirk stood up, she didn't move. Something was going on. A pissing contest, she thought, and it pissed her off that she was in the middle of it. Just as she was going to turn over whatever the hell was going on to the other officers standing around, a woman, a very beautiful and elegant woman, sat down when her son did.

"Mom, don't kill her." She glared at Toby and then asked him what he was doing. "I thought that since we more than likely won't be allowed to come back here anymore that I'd throw us a big party. This lady here, her name is Lander, I think she said, found me in line. I wouldn't have talked to her, but she's with this monster of a man, too, and I'm sort of afraid of him. He's filling up his plate along with hers."

"Toby, do you know that we're going to have to be here for a bit? I killed a man." He ate a chicken leg while he answered her. "I guess I need to practice more on knowing who is who then. No, I didn't know she was a vampire." She looked around at the open window shades. "How sure are you about that?"

"He's very sure. Why are you eating a salad when there is all this other food up there? I saw they had pudding. I love that stuff." She told the woman, not having any idea why she was what she'd been thinking about a salad. "How long have you two been on the road? I'm assuming it's been a while, right?"

"I was an infant when I was with her. She'd only just graduated from trucking college, and my mom and dad wanted to go out to a fancy dinner." Toby told the table the rest of the story, how he'd been with her and not dead when their bruin had been ambushed. When he pushed away his food, he looked at her. "If not for her all these years, sixteen on the road, I don't think that I'd be half the person that I am. I've called her mom from the start, and I don't know if I'd ever do anything different. She saved me."

No one said anything, and when the large man sat with them, he was talking to men and women in flak jackets with FBI and other initials on them when another woman sat down at the table. Toby, smiling, volunteered to go up and get another few plates of food when asked and came back with her a cup of hot tea. She really needed it about now.

Taking a lot less time than she thought that it might have, she was free to leave the bloodied table and enjoy some dessert. Not that she wanted any. She'd only been able to eat the salad because she'd been bullied into it. When Toby sat down next to her at the cleaned table, she hugged him to her.

"Did you want to hang out with Mr. Kirk?" He said that he was planning a play date, no. "I don't know how that works. For all I know, you guys go around sniffing each other's asses all the time, and that's how you know each other."

"I promise you, there is no butt-sniffing. And Mr. Kirk isn't a real bear. He's friends with someone powerful, and they gifted him immortality. There's more to it than that, I'm sure, but for now, I'm ready when you are to get on the road." She didn't move but stared at him. "What?"

"Something happened? Did one of them…that woman, Lander, did she push you into something or say something to you? Where is she?" He pushed her back in the chair when she started after the woman. "Toby, you're all I have. I have to protect you."

"I don't know if you've noticed it or not, but I'm about a foot taller than you are and outweigh you by a good fifty or so pounds. And I can shift into a big black bear." She felt her eyes fill again. "Don't do that. If you do, then the two of us will be blubbering all over each other, and we'll not be able to find us a place to sleep tonight."

"I can cry. They said that we can sleep on the lot tonight." He held her to his chest, and she sobbed. It terrified her every time something out of the ordinary happened, and he might get hurt. "Your parents would have been so proud of you, honey. You know that, don't you?"

"I do. Even though I never had any memories with them, you've brought them alive for me every time we talk about them. Even if you're just — that's it, isn't it? I completely forgot. Today would have been her birthday." She nodded and tried very hard to keep herself under control for a few seconds. "Ah, Mom. You're the best. I don't think in all the world that anyone could have ended up with a better role model than what I've had all these years."

They ended up leaving the lot and finding them a nice little camping area. They no longer shared a tent, but she knew that he was close by. Just as she was coming back from the shower, a very much needed one, she saw that there was a large jeep in their spot. She didn't have to reach out to Toby to figure out what was going on. He was standing by the car, talking to a man next to him. It turned out to be Mr. Kirk.

He enjoyed talking to the young man. Toby was personable as well as polite. Kirk thought that he was smart, too, but he, for some reason, kept it under his hat about that. When Dill, his aunt, joined them after changing into something less *jammie,* she called it, he thought that he could have stayed there forever.

"Why are you here?" He nearly laughed at her but didn't. She seemed to be on edge about something. It could have been the shooting, but he wasn't positive that was all of it. "You got all your delivery. The cops were taken care of. Though I will admit that it was nice seeing someone of authority get their comeuppance. So, again, why are you here? Toby and I aren't the kind of people men like you socialize with."

"I don't even want to hazard a guess at what you might mean by that. However, you're right. It is nice seeing the bad guys get what they deserve. But I'm here because I've been enjoying myself. Both this afternoon and now." Toby told his aunt to chill. "No, don't tell her that. She's just protecting herself and you. And from what I've seen, she's done a good job of both. No, I'm a wealthy man who doesn't get to hang out with someone around a campfire. Ever, I don't think. But even with all the crap going on today, I've really enjoyed your company. By the way, did you open the envelope? I was asked by my secretary to remind you about it?"

"It was something from my attorney." She'd opened it in the bathroom in case it was bad news. "It's all fine."

Brad didn't think it was anything near all fine, but he nodded. "I swear to you, Becka, I have no other motives here but to have a nice relaxing evening with a couple of nice people." She stood up, and he did as well. "Did I say something wrong?"

"No. I'm tired. I have a long drive tomorrow, and I have to get up early enough to go and get my trailer from the lot." She hugged Toby, then told him thanks for the food, and she was gone. She told Toby not to stay up too late. He had homework.

"You online school?" Toby said that he was a freshman in college and was taking a few classes through the summer. "Good job on that."

The two of them sat there for another two hours, just talking. He really didn't want to go home. And thought very seriously about driving a few spaces away and sleeping in his car so that he could—

"Mr. Kirk, my aunt made sure when I was younger to have spent time with a burin. She did it because I'm a bear, and I had questions that she didn't know. My dad changed my mom when they met so the two of them could run the burin together. I got a lot of questions answered while there, and I'd like to think I'm a bit more knowledgeable than most. All right?" Brad said that she'd been smart for doing that. Even though he'd been gifted a lot of magic and other things from a powerful burin, he knew very little about them. "Yeah, I kind of got that. You don't know crap if you don't mind me saying so."

Brad laughed a little, and the two of them sat there for a little while longer before he realized that he was staring at Becka's tent again. He'd been thinking all kinds of odd thoughts about her since she'd gone to bed. When Toby said his name, he looked at the young man.

"I don't want to upset you none here, but you're my aunt's mate. You know that, don't you?" Brad laughed, thinking that this was a good joke that the kid had. "I'm not kidding you, Mr. Kirk. I could smell it on the two of you. She won't figure it out either unless I tell her, but I think that you need to be told. Before someone else tells you. I have a feeling that the people with you today would make fun of you for not figuring it out on your own."

"Yes. Relentlessly." He looked at Becka's tent and then at Toby again. "How sure are you about this? As you've already said, I don't know crap."

"You're her mate. She's not going to be happy and come to you with open arms like some other woman might. She's been hurt. Still is if I don't miss my bet. This man, I don't know his name other than Danny, has been — it's why we travel and do not have a space of our own. He's been...I've never told her this, and I won't unless I have to, but when her home burnt to the ground, I could smell him and the others then. Then, about five years ago, I noticed his scent around the truck and cab, too. He's trying to get in." He felt his need to protect the two of them roar up. "Calm it down, or she'll come out here. She's got a bit of magic; she can talk to me when necessary, but she can also feel me when I get stressed. And you're stressing me a little."

"I'm assuming that's part of the mate stuff." Toby smiled at him and nodded. "I didn't know. I mean, I've been thinking about her a lot, but I thought

I was just enjoying her company. Which I am. Both of you. But this mating information? It's nothing that I thought of."

"I think I figured that out, too." They both laughed, and he felt better for it. "Those people you were with today, one of them smelled of bear. I know that none of them were bears, but they've had close contact with one. Do you know that person, too?"

"I do. I've only just met him. Well, the two of them. One is his mate, the other is a friend of ours. It's Calhoun Meyer. Have you heard of him?" Toby stared at him with an open mouth. "I'm going to take that as a yes. He's the king of the bruins."

"I know that. Every bear knows that, too." Toby leaned back in his chair and looked about as shell-shocked as he was feeling about finding out that he had a mate. "I don't want to tell you what to do here, but that man is wanting something from my aunt. If you can protect her, then I'm going to…do you really know King Meyer?"

"I do. Would you like to meet him?" Toby nodded, then shook his head so many times Brad didn't know what he wanted. "He can do that pop-in thing. If I call him here, he'll…I don't know what he'll do, actually. As I said, I've only just met him."

They talked for a bit longer. When Toby said he was going to hit the bed, Kirk asked if he could sit there for a bit longer. Telling him to just be careful had him shaking hands with the young man. He really was a good kid. It wasn't until he exhausted every question and gotten no answers he had about mates that he knew he reached out to the only other person that he'd come to think of as his best friend. Hamish would have answers. If he didn't, then he'd know where to get them.

Getting into his car, he did what he'd been thinking. Drove to a few empty spaces down and pulled into the lot. While sitting there, he tried to reason with himself and tell himself that she was going to be all right until morning. But it didn't work. Brad was worried for his new little family now, and it would be the same in the morning.

After reaching out to his friend, he told him everything. Not just the fact that he had to be told she was his mate but about the man trying to get into her rig. Then, when he thought that he'd exhausted himself, he told him again how much he'd enjoyed talking to the two of them and hadn't any idea that he'd just found her and that she had him a son.

"I'd not start out with that if I were you." He

asked which part when Hamish just showed up in the front seat of his car. "None of it. I mean, you'll tell her sometime, but I'd hold off about how her nephew had to tell you about her. Women can be touchy about the strangest things. Don't tell her that either. That will get us both in hot water."

"There seems to be a lot of things about women that scare you, too. Are you sure that you're the big badassed vamp, or is it, Lander?" He didn't even hesitate and said it was all Lander. "You're off your head if you ask me. And not all that helpful. The sixteen-year-old kid was more helpful than you are being."

"Then go wake him up so that you piss off his aunt." They both sat there for several seconds before they laughed. "Lander did some research on the two of them. When I left her, she was still digging. She told me about the murder and killing at the burin. The burin has since been taken apart. She didn't know why and said she'd get with Calhoun in the morning. That's all I can tell you about that. Becka is pretty much an open book, she said. There is nothing in her closet, it seems. I know that when I tell her about Becka being your mate, she'll dig deeper. Not that I think she'll find anything else."

"This is the strangest thing that has ever happened to me." They both sat there, staring into the darkness. "She's very beautiful. Smart and has done a better than average job on...how do I tell if what Toby told me is right? I mean, what if he's mistaken?"

"Do you feel like he might be?" Brad shook his head. "Then I'd take what he said as gospel. Hang on. I'm talking to Lander."

While his friend spoke to his mate, Brad got out of the car. He should have put her up in a hotel when he realized how chilly it was outside. But the two of them, she and Toby, seemed to be thrilled with camping out. Toby told him that it was nice to be able to have nature right there with them. He loved that part, too, but in small doses. He wasn't sure how he felt about camping out in the woods. He liked his comforts and didn't think he'd like doing this night after night.

Smiling, he told himself that he'd get used to it if that was what it took to make her happy. Brad laughed. Christ, he was getting to be as sappy as his friends with mates. He couldn't wait to figure out the other things that he'd heard about over the centuries. Also, he would have to figure out a way to tell her how old he was, too. That, he thought, was one of the many things that he'd put off as he'd been advised. But he would ask his son too when he —

"Lander wants to talk to you." He nodded and got back into the car. Whatever advice she had for him, he'd use it. She was a good deal smarter than her mate, as he knew Becka would be to him.

Before You Go...

HELP AN AUTHOR

write a review

THANK YOU!

Share your voice and help guide other readers to these wonderful books. Even if it's only a line or two, your reviews help readers discover the author's books so they can continue creating stories that you'll love. Log in to your favorite retailer and leave a review. Thank you.

AWARD WINNING, BESTSELLING AUTHOR

Kathi Barton, a winner of the Pinnacle Book Achievement Award and a best-selling author on Amazon and All Romance books, lives in Nashport, Ohio, with her husband, Paul. When not creating new worlds and romance, Kathi and her husband enjoy camping and going to auctions. She can also be seen at county fairs with her husband, an artist and potter.

Her muse, a cross between Jimmy Stewart and Hugh Jackman, brings her stories to life for her readers in a way that has them coming back time and again for more. Her favorite genre is paranormal romance, with a great deal of spice. You can visit Kathi online and drop her an email if you'd like. She loves hearing from her fans. aaronskiss@gmail.com.

Follow Kathi on her blog: http://kathisbartonauthor.blogspot.com/

www.ingramcontent.com/pod-product-compliance
Lightning Source LLC
Chambersburg PA
CBHW032009170626
46807CB00006B/2721